GOD
SAVE
THE
MARK

GOD
SAVE
THE
MARK

A NOVEL OF
CRIME AND CONFUSION

Donald E. Westlake

A TOM DOHERTY ASSOCIATES BOOK
NEW YORK

GOD SAVE THE MARK: A NOVEL OF CRIME AND CONFUSION

Copyright © 1967, 1995 by Donald E. Westlake

Introduction copyright © 2004 by Otto Penzler

This book is printed on acid-free paper.

Edited by Otto Penzler

Design by Milenda Nan Ok Lee

A Forge Book
Published by Tom Doherty Associates, LLC
175 Fifth Avenue
New York, NY 10010

www.tor.com

Forge® is a registered trademark of Tom Doherty Associates, LLC.

Library of Congress Cataloging-in-Publication Data

Westlake, Donald E.
    God save the mark : a novel of crime and confusion / Donald
Westlake.—1st Forge ed.
        p.   cm.
    "A Tom Doherty Associates book."
    ISBN 0-765-30918-1 (hc) (acid-free paper)
    ISBN 0-765-30919-X (pbk)
    1. Inheritance and succession—Fiction.   2. Murder victims'
families—Fiction.   3. Swindlers and swindling—Fiction. 4. New York
(N.Y.)—Fiction.   I. Title.

    PS3573.E9G59   2004
    813'.54—dc22

                                                                2003049426

Originally published in 1967 by Random House, Inc.

First Forge Edition: January 2004

Printed in the United States of America

0 9 8 7 6 5 4 3 2 1

To Nedra

Forgetting those things which are behind,
and reaching forth unto those things which are before,
I press toward the mark.

THE EPISTLE OF PAUL TO THE PHILIPPIANS

You must make your mark.

HORATIO ALGER

Introduction
by Otto Penzler

If there is a thematic thread running in its complex weave through the works of Donald E. Westlake, it is the notion of really bad luck, or, as he once stated it, bewilderment. Not the author's, mind you, but the trials he sets for his relentlessly challenged characters.

In the hard-boiled novels under the pseudonym Richard Stark, he writes about a very professional and totally amoral thief, Parker, whose plans seem all too frequently to go awry. Meticulously planned bank jobs and other sure-thing robberies have the nasty habit of being thwarted because of unforeseen circumstances that force him to work twice as hard for his money (well, okay, it's not really *his* money).

Still, the misfortunes that befall the gritty Parker are dwarfed by the cataclysmic ill fortune that clings to John Archibald Dortmunder like week-old egg yolk to an unwashed plate. His first caper, *The Hot Rock* (1970), actually began its life as a Parker novel. The idea was to steal a fabulously valuable gem—which, thanks to a swell plan, was achieved. And then it was lost. After it was recovered, it was lost again. And then Dortmunder and his little gang had to break *into* prison so that they could break *out* one of their cronies. And then the damned stone was gone again. By which time it was no longer just bad luck any more, but bad luck of such enormity, of such overwhelming inevitability, that it became funny.

Parker, for whatever strengths he may have, is not funny. Not even a little bit. And the Stark novels, with their many strengths, are not funny. Dortmunder doesn't *mean* to be funny—he actually has very well-thought-out thievery plans—but he is. Westlake's most popular character was, therefore, born, albeit against his will.

The Hot Rock was not, however, Westlake's first humorous book. He had started out as a hard-boiled writer, in the vein of Dashiell Hammett and Ernest Hemingway, with *The Mercenaries* (1960), *Killing Time* (1961), *361* (1962), and *Killy* (1963). The first Parker novel, *The Hunter*, was published in 1962.

The comic career (I mean the comic-*writing* career) for which Westlake is best known began with *The Fugitive Pigeon* in 1965. At that time, there were virtually no authors of humorous mystery fiction. Craig Rice had died, and Stuart Palmer, whose Hildegarde Withers adventures had been a light-hearted mainstay of page and screen for more than thirty years, had stopped writing. The common publishing wisdom then (and now, too, for that matter) was that humor doesn't sell. When *The Fugitive Pigeon* sold twice as many copies as any of his previous books, Westlake thought he might be on to something and followed it with the further hilarious exploits of put-upon protagonists in *The Busy Body* (1966), *The Spy in the Ointment* (1966), and *God Save the Mark* (1967), which won the Edgar Allan Poe Award of the Mystery Writers of America—forever winning the hearts of fellow crime writers by delivering the shortest acceptance speech in the history of the organization (or probably *any* organization, come to think of it): "I don't speak," he said. "I write. Thank you."

The Westlakian hallmark runs through all these sidesplitting novels. In *The Fugitive Pigeon*, two thugs show up to kill Charlie Poole (exchanging dialogue lifted unapologetically from Hemingway's short story "The Killers"). Charlie is not a fellow who has any reason to expect to be killed. He runs his uncle's bar, makes a modest living, and reads cheap fiction when in his apartment above the bar when he's off-duty. It's a quiet, kind of boring life, and he likes it that way. "I was born a bum," be says, "and I've been a bum for twenty-four years, and if it wasn't for my uncle AJ and this job running this bar, I would starve to death in a minute." So when a tough guy points a gun at him, Charlie is bewildered.

The maguffin in *The Busy Body* is the corpse of a gangster or, more accurately, the suit in which he was buried. A cache of heroin has been sewn into the lining. When Al Engel, a not-very-hard-working member of the organization that wants the suit, is told to dig up the coffin, get the suit (actually, just the jacket), and return the body to its peaceful resting place, he figures it shouldn't be too hard. Al's mother had wanted him to go to college, "Not to be a bum all your life," she said, "like your old man, the bum." So right after high school, Al went to his father and said, "Introduce me to somebody, Dad. I want to go to work for the organization." Al had no idea how much bad luck could befall someone chasing the most peripatetic body anyone has ever tried to pin down.

In *The Spy in the Ointment*, a Greenwich Village pacifist, entirely against his desires, finds himself a member of a league of assassins—partially because of a typographical error and partially because the Federal Bureau of Investigation insists on it. The utterly helpless hero is unexpectedly confronted by a man who tells him, "J. Eugene Raxford has no importance, is nothing and less than nothing."

"Well," responds Mr. Raxford in an internal monologue, "I'd thought and voiced and even written exactly the same sentiment myself more than once the last thirteen years, but hearing it spoken directly to my face by a total stranger was something else again." Yet another bewildering moment for a Westlake character caught in a large, sticky web.

It is with Fred Fitch, the hero (could anyone reasonably call him that?) of *God Save the Mark,* that the hapless loser reached its apotheosis. He is a sucker, a victim, a mark of such prodigious gullibility that the most inept grifter can easily bilk him at will. What's more, pathetic Fred knows it.

"Con men take one look at me," he laments, "streamline their pitches, and soon go gaily off to steak dinners while poor Fred Fitch sits at home and once again dines on gnawed fingernails. I have enough worthless receipts and bad checks to paper my living room, I own miles of tickets to nonexistent raffles and ball games and dances and clambakes and shivarees, my closet is full of little machines that stopped working miracles as soon as the seller went away, and I'm apparently on just about every sucker mailing list in the Western Hemisphere." In private, he girds himself and is sure he'll never be swindled again, but it happens so regularly that he has become friends with the cops at the Bunco Squad. "I find it impossible to believe," he says, "that anyone could lie to another human being to his face."

The scam that opens the book was a gift from Westlake's former college roommate. He called the author to tell him of the rotten guy who had just cheated him out of money by claiming to have a C.O.D. package for his neighbor, who was not at home. He paid for the (empty) parcel and brought it to his neighbor who, of course, knew nothing about it. Naturally,

Westlake commiserated, but (and this is what separates authors from the rest of us) immediately said to himself, "Hey, I can use this!"

Poor Fred (and that is about the only way one can think of him) is a typical protagonist of a Westlake comic novel. Whether that character is a crook or a victim, it is difficult not to root for him, to hope that, somehow, against all odds, things will work out for him. They either don't deserve what is happening to them because they are essentially innocent, or they deserve better in their endeavors because they have created an excellent plan, entirely lacking in malice or violence, that inevitably fails. Consequently, it is easy to relate to them because most of us have, at one time or another, felt victimized, and, at another time or another, felt that our perfectly laid plans went terribly agley.

No matter how frustrated, agonized, disappointed, humiliated, irritated, or pained poor Fred (or the other dim stars in Westlake's galaxy) becomes, they never descend into extremes of behavior by resorting to savagery or by abandoning all hope. Thus they remain comic characters, not cartoon characters. They retain their humanity. That is why they, and Donald E. Westlake, will be around for as long as people read books.

GOD
SAVE
THE
MARK

ONE

Friday the nineteenth of May was a full day. In the morning I bought a counterfeit sweepstakes ticket from a one-armed man in a barbershop on West 23rd Street, and in the evening I got a phone call at home from a lawyer saying I'd just inherited three hundred seventeen thousand dollars from my Uncle Matt. I'd never heard of Uncle Matt.

As soon as the lawyer hung up I called my friend Reilly of the Bunco Squad at his house in Queens. "It's me," I said. "Fred Fitch."

Reilly sighed and said, "What have they done to you this time, Fred?"

"Two things," I said. "One this morning and one just now."

"Better watch yourself, then. My grandma always said troubles come in threes."

"Oh, my Lord," I said. "Clifford!"

"What's that?"

"I'll call you back," I said. "I think the third one already came."

I hung up and went downstairs and rang Mr. Grant's bell. He came to the door with a large white napkin tucked under his chin and holding a small fork upright in his hand, a tiny curled shrimp impaled on it. Which was a case of sweets to the sweet, Mr. Grant being a meek curled-shrimp of a man himself, balding, given to spectacles with steel rims, employed as a history teacher at some high school over in Brooklyn. We met at the mailboxes every month or so and exchanged anonymities, but other than that our social contact was nil.

I said, "Excuse me, Mr. Grant, I know it's dinnertime, but do you have a new roommate named Clifford?"

He blanched. Fork and shrimp drooped in his hand. He blinked very slowly.

Knowing it was hopeless, I went on anyway, saying, "Pleasant-looking sort, about my age, crewcut, white shirt open at the collar, tie loose, dark slacks." Over the years I've grown rather adept at giving succinct descriptions, unfortunately. I would have gone on and given estimates of Clifford's height and weight but I doubted they were needed.

They weren't. Shrimp at half-mast, Mr. Grant said to me, "I thought he was *your* roommate."

"He said there was a COD package," I said.

Mr. Grant nodded miserably. "Me, too."

"He didn't have enough cash in the apartment."

"He'd already borrowed some from Wilkins on the second floor."

I nodded. "Had a fistful of crumpled bills in his left hand."

Mr. Grant swallowed bile. "I gave him fifteen dollars."

I swallowed bile. "I gave him twenty."

Mr. Grant looked at his shrimp as though wondering who'd put it on his fork. "I suppose," he said slowly, "I suppose we ought to . . ." His voice trailed off.

"Let's go talk to Wilkins," I said.

"All right," he said, and sighed, and came out to the hall, shutting the door carefully after himself. We went on up to the second floor.

This block of West 19th Street consisted almost entirely of three- and four-story buildings with floor-through apartments sporting fireplaces, back gardens, and high ceilings, and how the entire block had so far missed the wrecker's sledge I had no idea. In our building, Mr. Grant had the first floor, a retired Air Force officer named Wilkins had the second, and I lived up top on the third. We all three were bachelors, quiet and sedentary, and not given to disturbingly loud noises. Of us, I was at thirty-one the youngest and Wilkins was much the oldest.

When Mr. Grant and I reached Wilkins' door, I rang the bell and we stood around with that embarrassed uneasiness always felt by messengers of bad tidings.

After a moment the door opened and there stood Wilkins, looking like the Correspondence Editor of the *Senior Citizens' Review.* He wore red sleeve garters with his blue shirt, a green eyeshade was squared off on his forehead, and in his ink-stained right hand he held an ancient fountain pen. He looked at me, looked at Mr. Grant, looked at Mr. Grant's napkin, looked at Mr. Grant's fork, looked at Mr. Grant's shrimp, looked back at me, and said, "Eh?"

I said, "Excuse me, sir, but did someone named Clifford come to see you this afternoon?"

"Your roommate," he said, pointing his pen at me. "Gave him seven dollars."

Mr. Grant moaned. Wilkins and I both looked at his shrimp, as though it had moaned. Then I said, "Sir, this man Clifford, or whatever his name is, he isn't my roommate."

"Eh?"

"He's a con man, sir."

"Eh?" He was squinting at me like a man looking across Texas at midday.

"A con man," I repeated. "Con means confidence. A confidence man. A sort of crook."

"Crook?"

"Yes, sir. A con man is someone who tells you a convincing lie, as a result of which you give him money."

Wilkins put his head back and looked at the ceiling, as though to stare through it into my apartment and see if Clifford weren't really there after all, in shirtsleeves, quietly going about the business of being my new roommate. But he failed to see him—or failed to see through the ceiling, I'm not sure which—and looked at me again, saying, "But what about the package? Wasn't it his?"

"Sir, there wasn't any package," I said. "That was the con. That is, the lie he told you was that there was a package, a COD package, and he—"

"Exactly," said Wilkins, pointing his pen at me with a little spray of ink, "exactly the word. COD. Cash on delivery."

"But there wasn't any package," I kept telling him. "It was a lie, to get money from you."

"No package? Not your roommate?"

"That's it, sir."

"Why," said Wilkins, abruptly outraged, "the man's a damn fraud!"

"Yes, sir."

"Where is he now?" Wilkins demanded, going up on tiptoe to look past my shoulder.

"Miles from here, I should think," I said.

"Do I get you right?" he said, glaring at me. "You don't even *know* this man?"

"That's right," I said.

"But he came from your apartment."

"Yes, sir. He'd just talked me into giving him twenty dollars."

Mr. Grant said, "I gave him fifteen." He sounded as mournful as the shrimp.

Wilkins said to me, "Did you think he was your roommate? Makes no sense at all."

"No, sir," I said. "He told me he was Mr. Grant's roommate."

Wilkins snapped a stern look at Mr. Grant. "Is he?"

"Of course not!" wailed Mr. Grant. "I gave him fifteen dollars myself!"

Wilkins nodded. "I see," he said. Then, thoughtfully, ruminatively, he said, "It seems to me we should contact the authorities."

"We were just about to," I said. "I thought I'd call my friend on the Bunco Squad."

Wilkins squinted again, under his eyeshade. "I beg your pardon?"

"It's part of the police force. The ones who concern themselves with the confidence men."

"You have a friend in this organization?"

"We met in the course of business," I said, "but over the years we've become personal friends."

"Then by all means," said Wilkins decisively. "I've never seen going through channels accomplish anything yet. Your friend it is."

So the three of us went on up to my place, Wilkins still wearing his eyeshade and carrying his pen, Mr. Grant still wearing his napkin and carrying his fork and shrimp. We entered the apartment and I offered them chairs but they preferred to stand. I called Reilly again, and as soon as I said who I was he said, "COD Clifford."

"What?"

"COD Clifford," he repeated. "I didn't connect the name at first, not till after you hung up. That's who it was, wasn't it?"

"It sounds about right," I said.

"He was some other tenant's new roommate."

"And a COD package had come."

"That's him, all right," Reilly said, and I could visualize him nodding at the telephone. He has a large head, with a thick mass of black hair and a thick bushy black mustache, and when he nods he does so with such judicious authority you can't help but believe he has just thought an imperishable truth. I sometimes think Reilly does so well with the Bunco Squad because he's part con man himself.

I said, "He got twenty dollars from me, fifteen from Mr. Grant on the first floor, and seven from Mr. Wilkins on the second."

Wilkins waved his pen at me, whispering hoarsely, "Make it twelve. For the official record, twelve."

Into the phone I said, "Mr. Wilkins says, for the official record make it twelve."

Reilly laughed while Wilkins frowned. Reilly said, "There's a touch of the con in everybody."

"Except me," I said bitterly.

"Some day, Fred, some psychiatrist is going to do a book on you and make you famous forever."

"Like Count Sacher-Masoch?"

I always make Reilly laugh. He thinks I'm the funniest sad sack he knows, and what's worse he tells me so.

Now he said, "Okay, I'll add your name to Clifford's sucker list, and when we get him you'll be invited to the viewing."

"Do you want a description?"

"No, thanks. We've got a hundred already, several with

points of similarity. Don't worry, we'll be getting this one. He works too much, he's pushing his luck."

"If you say so." In my experience, which is extensive, the professional workers of short cons don't usually get caught. Which is nothing against Reilly and the others of the Bunco Squad, but merely reflects the impossibility of the job they've been given. By the time they arrive at the scene of the crime, the artist is invariably gone and the sucker usually isn't even sure exactly what happened. Aside from dusting the victim for fingerprints, there really isn't much the Reillys can do.

This time he had me give him my fellow pigeons' full names, assured me once again that our complaint would go into the bulging Clifford file downtown, and then he asked me, "Now, what else?"

"Well," I said, somewhat embarrassed to be telling about this in front of my neighbors, "this morning a one-armed man in a barbershop on West—"

"Counterfeit sweepstakes ticket," he said.

"Reilly," I said, "how is it you know all these people but you never catch any?"

"We got the Demonstration Kid, didn't we? And Slim Jim Foster? And Able Mabel?"

"All right," I said.

"Your one-armed man, now," Reilly said, "that's Wingy St. Charles. How come you tipped so soon?"

"This afternoon," I said, "I suddenly got a suspicion, you know the way I always do, five hours too late."

"I know," he said. "God, how I know."

"So I went up to the Irish Tourist Board office on East 50th Street," I said, "and showed it to a man there, and he said it was a fake."

"And you bought it this morning. Where?"

"In a barbershop on West 23rd Street."

"Okay. It's soon enough, he might still be working the same neighborhood. We've got a chance. Not a big chance, but a chance. Now, what else do you have?"

"When I came home," I said, "the phone was ringing. It was a man said he was a lawyer, Goodkind, office on East 38th Street. Said I'd just inherited three hundred seventeen thousand dollars from my Uncle Matt."

"Did you check with the family? Is Uncle Matt dead?"

"I don't have any Uncle Matt."

"Okay," said Reilly. "This one we get for sure. When do you go to his office?"

"Tomorrow morning, ten o'clock."

"Right. We'll give it five minutes. Give me the address."

I gave him the address, he said he'd see me in the morning, and we both hung up.

My guests were both staring at me, Mr. Grant in amazement and Wilkins with a sort of fixed ferocity. It was Wilkins who said, "Lot of money, that."

"What money?"

"Three hundred thousand dollars." He nodded at the phone. "What you're getting."

"But I'm not getting three hundred thousand dollars," I said. "It's another con game, like Clifford."

Wilkins squinted. "Eh? How's that follow?"

Mr. Grant said, "But if they give you the money . . ."

"That's just it," I said. "There isn't any money. It's a racket."

Wilkins cocked his head to one side. "Don't see it," he said. "Don't see where they make a profit."

"There's a thousand ways," I said. "For instance, they might talk me into putting all the money into a certain investment, where my so-called Uncle Matt had it, but there's a tax problem or transfer costs and they can't touch the capital without endangering the whole investment, so I have to get two or three thousand dollars in cash from somewhere else to pay the expenses. Or the money's in some South American country and we have to pay the inheritance tax in cash from here before they'll let the money out. There's a new gimmick every day, and ten new suckers to try it on."

"Barnum," suggested Wilkins. "One born a minute, two to take him."

"Two," I said, "is a conservative number."

Mr. Grant said, faintly, "Does this happen to you all the time?"

"I couldn't begin to tell you," I said.

"But why you?" he asked. "This is the first time anything like this ever happened to me. Why should it happen to you so much?"

I couldn't answer him. There just wasn't a single thing I could say in response to a question like that. So I stood there and looked at him, and after a while he and Wilkins went away, and I spent the evening thinking about the question Mr. Grant had asked me, and trying out various answers I might have given him, ranging from, "I guess that's just the breaks of the game," to, "Drop dead," and none of them was really satisfactory.

TWO

I suppose it all began twenty-five years ago, when I returned home from my first day of kindergarten without my trousers. I did have the rather vague notion they'd been traded to some classmate, but I couldn't remember what had been given to me in exchange, nor did I seem to have anything in my possession that hadn't already belonged to me when I'd left for school, a younger and happier child, at nine that morning. Nor was I sure of the identity of the con infant who had done me in, so that neither he nor my trousers were ever found.

From that day forward my life has been an endless series of belated discoveries. Con men take one look at me, stream-line their pitches, and soon go gaily off to steak dinners while poor Fred Fitch sits at home and once again dines on gnawed fingernail. I have enough worthless receipts and bad checks to paper my living room, I own miles of tickets to nonexistent raffles and ball games and dances and clambakes and shivarees, my closet is full of little machines that stopped working mir-acles as soon as the seller went away, and I'm apparently on just about every sucker mailing list in the Western Hemisphere.

I really don't know why this should be true. I am not the typical mark, or victim, not according to Reilly or to all the books I've read on the subject. I am not greedy, nor uneducated, nor particularly stupid, nor an immigrant unfamiliar with the language and customs. I am only—but it is enough—gullible. I find it impossible to believe that anyone could lie to another human being to his face. It has happened to me hundreds of times already, but for some reason I remain unconvinced. When I am alone I am strong and cynical and unendingly suspicious, but as soon as the glib stranger appears in front of me and starts his spiel my mind disappears in a haze of belief. The belief is all-encompassing; I may be the only person in New York City in the twentieth century with a money machine.

This endless gullibility has, of course, colored my entire life. I left my hometown in Montana to come to New York City at the very early age of seventeen, much sooner than I would have preferred if it had not been that I was surrounded at home by friends and relatives all of whom had seen me played for a fool more often than I could count. It was embarrassment that drove me from my home to the massive anonymity of New York, when otherwise I might have stayed forever within ten blocks of the place of my birth.

My relationship with women has also been affected, and badly. Since high school I have avoided any but the most casual acquaintance with the opposite sex, and all because of my gullibility. In the first place, any girl who became close friends with me would sooner or later—probably sooner—see me humiliated by a passing bunco artist. In the second place, were I to grow more than fond of a particular girl, how could I ever really know her opinion of me? She might say she loved me, and when she was saying it I would believe her, but an hour later, a day later . . .

No. Solitude has its dreary aspects, but they don't include self-torture.

Similarly my choice of occupation. Not for me the gregarious office job, side by side with my mates, typing or writing or thinking away in our companionable white-shirted tiers. Solitude was the answer here as well, and for the past eight years I have been a freelance researcher, numbering among my clients many writers and scholars and television producers, for whom I plumb the local libraries in search of specific knowledge.

So here I was at thirty-one, a confirmed bachelor and a semirecluse, with all the occupational diseases of my sedentary calling: round shoulders and round spectacles and round stomach and round forehead. I seemed inadvertently to have found the way to skip the decades, to go from the middle twenties to the middle fifties and there to stay while the gray years drifted silently by and nothing broke the orderly flow of time but the occasional ten-dollar forays of passing confidence men.

Until, on that Friday the nineteenth of May, I received the phone call from the lawyer named Goodkind that changed—and very nearly ended—my life.

THREE

In an effort to eliminate, or at least contain, my pot belly, I've taken to walking as much as possible whenever I go out, and so on Saturday morning I walked from my apartment on West 19th Street to the office of the alleged lawyer, Goodkind, on East 38th Street. I made one stop along the way, in a drugstore on the corner of West 23rd and Sixth Avenue, where I purchased a packet of tobacco.

I'd gone half a block farther up Sixth Avenue when I heard someone behind me call, "Say, you!" I turned, and a tall and rather heavy-set man was striding toward me, motioning at me to stay where I was. He wore a dark suit, the jacket flapping open, a white shirt bunched at the waist, and a wrinkled brown tie. He looked like an ex-Marine who has only recently started to get flabby.

When he reached me he said, "You just bought some tobacco in the store on the corner, right?"

"Yes, I did," I said. "Why?"

He pulled his wallet from his hip pocket and flipped it open to show me his badge. "Police," he said. "All we want you to do is cooperate."

"I'll be happy to," I said, with that sudden flutter of guilt we all feel when abruptly confronted by the law.

He said, "What sort of bill did you use back there?"

"What sort? You mean—? Well, it was a five."

He pulled a crumpled bill from his jacket pocket and handed it to me, saying, "This one?"

I looked at the bill, but of course there's no way to tell one piece of money from another, so eventually I had to say, "I guess it is. I can't be sure."

"Take a close look at it, brother," he said, and he suddenly sounded much tougher than before.

I took a close look, but how did I know if this was the bill I'd used or not? "I'm sorry," I said, feeling very nervous about it, "but I just can't be positive one way or the other."

"The counterman says you're the one passed it on him," he said.

I looked at him, saw him glowering at me. I said, "Passed it on him? You mean it's counterfeit?"

"That's exactly right," he said.

"It's happened again," I said, sadly studying the bill in my hand. "People pass counterfeit money on me all the time."

"Where'd you get this one?"

"I'm sorry, I just don't know."

I could tell by his face that he was somewhat suspicious of me, and he confirmed it by saying, "You don't seem too anxious to cooperate, brother."

"Oh, I am," I said. "It's just I don't remember where I got this particular bill."

"Come over to the car," he said, and led me to a battered green unmarked Plymouth parked near a fireplug. He had me get in on the passenger side in front, and then he came around and slid in behind the wheel. A police radio under the dashboard was crackling and giving occasional spurts of words.

The detective said, "Let's see some identification."

I showed him my library and Social Security cards, and he carefully wrote down my name and address in a black notebook. He'd taken the five-dollar bill back by now, and he wrote its serial number on the same page, then said to me, "You got any more bills on you?"

"Yes, I do."

"Let's see."

I had thirty-eight dollars in bills, two tens, three fives and three ones. I gave them to him and he studied each of them at length, holding them up to the light, rubbing them between thumb and finger, listening to them crinkle, and then putting them atop the dashboard in two piles.

When he was done, it turned out three more of them had been counterfeit, a ten and two fives. "We'll have to impound these," he said, and gave me the other bills back. "I'll give you a receipt, but of course you know you can't collect good money for these. If there's ever a conviction based on these bills it's possible you'll be able to make a partial recovery from the people who made them, but otherwise I'm afraid you've been had."

"That's all right," I said, and grinned weakly. In the first place, I was used to being had, and in the second place, I was delighted that he no longer thought I was potentially a member of the gang passing them.

He had a receipt book in the glove compartment. He got it out and wrote out an involved receipt, including the serial numbers of the bills, and when he handed it to me he said, "You want to be more careful from now on. Look at your change when it's given to you and you won't make these costly mistakes."

"I'll do that," I promised. I got out of the car, looked at my watch, and saw I'd have to move fast if I intended to reach Goodkind's office by ten o'clock. I began walking briskly uptown.

I reached 32nd Street before it occurred to me I'd been taken. Then I stood stock-still on the sidewalk, and as I felt the blood drain from my head, I took out the receipt and looked at it.

Twenty dollars. I had just bought this scribbled piece of paper for twenty dollars.

I turned around and ran, but of course by the time I got to 24th Street he was long gone. I started looking around for a phone booth, intending to call Reilly at Headquarters, but then I remembered I'd be seeing him at the supposed lawyer's office a little after ten.

A little after ten? I looked at my watch and it was just one minute before the hour. I was supposed to be there now!

I flagged a cab, which meant another dollar the bogus policeman had cost me. I got into the back seat, the driver started the meter, and we raced uptown directly into the middle of the garment center's perpetual traffic jam.

I got to Goodkind's office at twenty after ten. The hallway and reception room and Goodkind's private office were all crawling with Bunco Squad men, who had sprung the trap before the cheese had arrived. I threaded my way through them, muttering hello to the ones I knew and identifying myself to the rest, and found Reilly in Goodkind's office with two other Bunco. Squad men and, seated at his desk, a hungry lupine sharpie with onyx eyes who had to be Goodkind himself.

Reilly said to me, "Where the hell have you been?"

"A phony policeman worked the counterfeit ploy on me for twenty dollars," I said.

"Oh, Christ," said Reilly, and suddenly looked too weary to stand.

Goodkind, grinning hungrily at me, said, in a voice like the one Eve must have heard from the serpent, "Hello there, Fred. It's really too bad you're my client."

I looked at him. "What?"

Reilly said, "He's legit, you goofball. He's on the up-and-up."

"You mean—?"

"What a suit I'd have against you," Goodkind said gleefully. "And you with all that money."

"It's square," Reilly told me. "You really did inherit three hundred and seventeen thousand dollars, and God help us all."

"Still," said Goodkind, rubbing his hands together, "maybe we can work something out."

I stretched out on the floor and became unconscious.

Four

Jack Reilly is a great bear of a man, sprinkled with pipe to-bacco. Two hectic hours after my subsidence on the floor of Attorney Goodkind's office, Reilly and I entered a bar on East 34th Street, and he said, "Fred, if you're going to drive me to drink, the least you can do is pay for it."

"I guess I can," I said. "Now." And my knees got weak again.

Reilly steered me to a booth in the back, hollered till a waitress came, ordered Jack Daniels on the rocks for both of us, and said to me, "If you'll take my advice, Fred, the first thing you'll do is get yourself another lawyer."

I said, doubtfully, "That doesn't seem fair, does it? After all, he's the one handling the estate."

"He handles it the way I handle my girl," he said, and made a fondling motion in the air. "Goodkind's a little too much in love with your money, Fred. Unload him."

"All right," I promised, though secretly I doubted if I had the nerve to just walk into Goodkind's office and fire him. But maybe I could hire another attorney and *he* could fire Good-kind.

Reilly said, "And the second thing you better do, Fred, is figure out a safe place to put that money."

"I'd rather not think about it," I said.

"Well, you've got to think about it," he told me. "I don't want you calling me every hundred dollars till it's gone."

"Let's talk about it later," I said. "After I've had a drink and a chance to calm down."

"It's an awful lot of money, Fred," he said.

I already knew that. It was three hundred and seventeen thousand dollars, give or take a nickel. Not only that, it was three hundred and seventeen thousand dollars *net*, after inheritance taxes and legal fees and all the rest of it, the actual amount of the inheritance being nearly five hundred thousand. Half a million.

Five million dimes.

It seems I really did have an Uncle Matt, or that is, a grand-uncle by that name. My great-grandmother on my mother's mother's side married twice and had one son by the second marriage, who in his turn had three wives but no children. (A quick phone call to my mother in Montana from Goodkind's office had garnered this information.) Uncle Matt, or Matthew Grierson, which was his real name, had spent most of his life as a ne'er-do-well and—presumably—alcoholic. Every single relative he had reviled him and snubbed him and refused him entry to their homes. Except me, of course. I never did an un-kind thing to Uncle Matt in my life, primarily because I'd never heard of him, my parents being too genteel to mention such a bad character in the presence of children.

But it was this kindness by default which had produced my windfall. Uncle Matt hadn't wanted to leave his money to a dog and cat hospital or a scholarship fund for underprivileged spastics, but he detested all his relations just as severely as they had all detested him. Except me. So it seems that Uncle Matt took an interest in me, studying me from afar, and decided that I was a loner like himself, cut off from the rotten family and living my own life the way I wanted. I don't know why he never introduced himself to me, unless he was afraid that close up I'd turn out to be as bad as the rest of his relations. At any rate he studied me, and thought he sensed some sort of affinity between us, and in the end he left his money to me.

The source of the money itself was a little confusing. Eight years ago Uncle Matt had gone off to Brazil with an unspecified amount of capital which he'd apparently saved over a long period of time, and three years later he'd come back from Brazil with over half a million dollars in cash and gems and securities. How he'd done it no one seemed to know. In fact, so far as my mother had been able to tell me over the phone, no one in the family had even known Uncle Matt was rich. As Mother said, "A lot of people would have treated Matt a heap different if they *had* known, believe you me."

I believed her.

In any case, Uncle Matt had spent the last three years living right here in New York City, in an apartment hotel on Central Park South. Twelve days ago he had died, had been buried without fanfare, and his will had been opened by his attorney, Marcus Goodkind. Among this document's instructions, it had commanded the attorney to complete all the possible legal rigmarole before informing me either of my uncle's death or of the bequest. "My nephew Fredric is of a sensitive and delicate nature," the will read on this point. "Funerals would give him the flutters and red tape would give him hives."

It had taken twelve days, and so far as I felt right now I

wished it had taken twelve years. Twelve hundred years. I sat in this booth with Reilly, a hundredthousandaire waiting for a Jack Daniels on the rocks, and all I felt was sick and terrified.

And there was worse to come. After the belated arrival of our drinks, and after I'd downed half of mine in the first swallow, Reilly said, "Fred, let's get this business of the money straightened away. I've got some other things to talk to you about."

"Like what?"

"The money first."

I leaned forward. "Like where the money came from?"

He seemed surprised. "Haven't you figured that out yet?"

"Figured it out? I don't get you."

"Fred, have you ever heard of Matt 'Short Sheet' Gray?"

The name rang a faint distant bell. I said, "Did Maurer write about him?"

"I don't know, he might. Midwest con man, over forty years. Spread a swath of receipts across the middle of the country as thick as fallen leaves in October."

I said, "My uncle's name was Matthew Grierson."

"So was Short Sheet's. Matt Gray was what you might call his professional name."

I reached unsteadily for my drink. Though it was half gone I still managed to slop some on my thumb. I drank what was left, licked my thumb, blinked at Reilly, and said, "I've inherited three hundred thousand dollars from a con man."

"And the question is," he said, "where's a good safe place for it."

"From a con man," I said. "Reilly, don't you get it?"

"Yeah yeah," he said impatiently. "Fred, this is serious."

I chuckled. "Talk about casting your bread on the waters," I said. I laughed. "A con man," I said. I guffawed. "I'm inheriting my own money back," I said. I whooped.

Reilly leaned across the table and slapped me across the face. "You're getting hysterical, Fred," he pointed out.

I was. I took two pieces of ice from my glass, put one in my mouth, and held the other against my stinging cheek where Reilly had given me his Irish hand. "I suppose I needed that," I said.

"You did."

"Then thanks."

The waitress came over, looking suspicious, and said, "Anything wrong here?"

"Yes," Reilly told her. "These drinks are empty."

She picked up the glasses, looked at us suspiciously some more, and went away.

Reilly said, "The point is, what are you going to do with the money?"

"Buy a gold brick with it, I suspect."

"Or the Brooklyn Bridge," Reilly agreed gloomily.

"Verrazano Narrows Bridge," I said. "Only the newest and most modern for my money."

"Where's the money now?" he asked me.

"The securities are in a couple of safe deposit boxes, the gems are in the Winston Company vault, and Uncle Matt had seven savings accounts in different banks around town. Plus a checking account. Plus he owned some property."

The waitress brought our fresh drinks, looked at us suspiciously, and went away again.

Reilly said, "The securities and gems are all right where they are. Just leave them there and have your lawyer switch the paperwork over to you. The cash we'll have to work out. There's got to be a way to keep you from getting your hands on it."

I said, "There was something else you wanted to talk to me about."

"You haven't had enough to drink yet," he said.

"Tell me now," I said.

"At least drink some of it," he said. "You'll spill it all over yourself."

"Tell me now," I insisted.

He shrugged. "Okay, buddy. A couple of people from Homicide are coming to see you at your home at four o'clock this afternoon."

"Who? Why?"

"Your Uncle Matt was murdered, Fred. Struck down with the well-known blunt instrument."

I poured cold Jack Daniels in my lap.

FIVE

Half an hour later, as I walked homeward through Madison Square Park, a girl with marzipan breasts flung herself into my arms, kissed me soundly, and whispered in my ear, "Pretend you know me!"

"Oh, come on," I said irritably, "how much of a fool do you think I am?" I pushed her roughly away.

"Darling!" she cried bravely, holding her arms out to me. "It's so good to see you again!" Panic gleamed in her eyes, and lines of tension marred her beautiful face.

Could it be real? After all, strange things do happen. And this was New York City, with the United Nations just a few blocks away. For all I knew, some sort of spy ring could—

No! For once in my life I had to remain the skeptic. And if this wasn't the opening shot of a variation on the badger game, I wasn't the good old Fred Fitch known and loved by grifters from coast to coast. ("After all," as Reilly had once said, "if they don't have songs about you, Fred, it's only because they don't sing.")

I said, "Young lady, you have made a mistake. I've never seen you before in my life."

"If you don't help me," she said rapidly under her breath, "I'll tear off my clothes and swear you attacked me."

"In Madison Square Park? At ten minutes to one in the afternoon?" I gestured at the hordes of lunch-munching office workers, pigeon-feeding widows, and autohypnotic retirees filling the benches and paths around us.

She looked around and shrugged. "Oh, well," she said. "It was a good try. Come on, Fred, let's go have a drink and talk it over."

"You know who I am?"

"Of course I know who you are. Didn't your Uncle Matt talk about you all the time? How he used to dandle you on his knee when you were no higher—"

"I never met Uncle Matt in my life," I said. "That one wasn't even a good try."

She got very irritated, put her hands on her hips, and said, "All right, smart guy. Do you want to know what's going on or don't you?"

"I don't." Although, of course, I did. The other half of gullibility is curiosity.

She stepped closer to me again, so close the marzipan nearly touched my shirtfront. "I'm on your side, Fred," she said softly. She began fingering my tie. Watching her fingers, looking both little-girlish and sexy, she murmured, "Your life's in danger, you know. Powerful interests in Brazil. The same ones who murdered your Uncle Matt."

"What's your part in all this?"

She looked quickly around and said, "Not here. Come to my place tonight—160 West 78th. Smith. Be there at nine."

"But what's it all about?"

"We can't be seen together," she said. "Too dangerous. To-night at nine." With which she spun away from me and walked briskly off toward Madison Avenue, her skirt twitching about her legs as she walked. Even the retirees on the benches roused themselves from their stupor enough to watch her walk by.

I murmured to myself, "160 West 78th," committing the address to memory. But then I shook my head, angry with myself; I was on the verge of falling into another trap. Forcing determination, I walked on southward, met with no further incidents, and found waiting on my doorstep as brassy a blonde as I ever want to see. If the other one had been made of marzipan, this one was made of pillows encased in steel. She looked like the model for all those cartoons about tough-looking broads being led into paddy wagons.

She'd been leaning against my door, arms folded—probably running through a few choruses of *Lili Marlene*—but when I arrived she straightened up, put her hands on her hips—that's two women who'd faced me that way in fifteen minutes—and said, "So you're the nephew, huh? You don't look like much."

"Don't start," I told her. "Whatever you're up to, I'm on the alert."

"I bet you look a lot like the milkman," she said. "I told Matt you were nothing but a fruit, but he wouldn't listen to me."

"A what?"

"A fruit," she said. "A fig. A fuzzy peach. An appery-cot."

"Now, look—"

"You look," she said, and opened a patent-leather black purse and handed me a letter. "Read that," she said.

My name was written on the envelope in a scrawling and shaky masculine hand. I took the letter and turned it around without opening it and said, "I suppose inside here there's a note purporting to be from my Uncle Matt."

"Purporting? What kind of word is that? You been seeing that fag lawyer?"

"You mean Goodkind?"

"That's the one. And never mind purporting, that letter's the jake."

"I'll do you a favor," I said. "I won't even open this letter. You just take it back and go on about your business. I won't turn you over to the police, and we'll just call it even."

"You're a sweetheart," she told me. "You're a goddam prince. Read the letter there while I find my violin."

"I'm not going to read it," I said, "and if I did read it I wouldn't believe it."

She looked at me with a very cold eye, and continued to stand in front of my door with arms akimbo. "Is that right?" she said.

"That's right," I said, expecting her any instant to go into a crouch and start throwing left jabs.

Instead, she pointed a scarlet-tipped finger at me and said, "Let me tell you something, honey. It'll take a better man than you to pull a fast one on little Gertie. You just better wise up."

"Little Gertie? Is that supposed to be you?"

"Oh, you are a one," she said. "Read the damn letter and quit fooling around."

"You really want to go through with this, do you?"

"Read the letter."

"All right. Excuse me one minute. Just step aside, there, I want to unlock the door."

She stepped aside, I unlocked the door, and we went into the apartment. "Oh, isn't this sweet," she said, looking around the living room. "Of course, it could use the masculine touch."

"Well, you'd be the one to give it," I said, and went over to the telephone.

She watched me for five seconds of surprise, and then she

barked with sudden laughter, saying, "Well, well, he's got a little sting in his little tail, hasn't he?" She tossed her patent-leather purse on the sofa—the sofa cringed away from it—and said, "You got anything to drink in here? I mean, besides peach brandy."

"You won't be staying that long," I said, and began to dial Reilly's office number.

"Don't make a complete horse's ass of yourself, honey," she said, strolling around the room and grimacing at my paintings. "Call Goodkind first and ask him about me. Gertie Divine, the Body Secular." She raised her arms above her head, half-turned toward me, and did a bump that caused a sonic boom.

She seemed so sure of herself. And yet, didn't they all seem sure of themselves? Hadn't the one-armed man, and Clifford, and this morning's phony cop?

Still, I'd already made one bad mistake, siccing Reilly on Goodkind. Was it possible that this was another? I stopped dialing Reilly's number, hung up, found the phone book, found Goodkind's number, and phoned him instead.

He was all oil. "Well, well, if it isn't my favorite client. Not to mention the man I'm about to sue for defamation of character. Heh, heh."

I said, "Have you ever heard of Gertie Divine?"

"What?" He sounded as startled as if I'd hit him with a cattle prod. "Where have you heard about her?"

"She's right here."

"Get her out of there! Don't listen to her, don't listen to a word she says! As your attorney, Fred, I urge you, I urge you vehemently, get that woman out of there this instant."

I said, "I really wish you wouldn't call me Fred."

"Get her out of there," he said, a bit more quietly. "That's the long and the short of it, get her out of there."

"She says she's got a letter from Uncle Matt," I said.

That set him off again. "Don't read it! Don't even touch it! Close your eyes, close your ears, get her out!"

"Should I call Reilly?"

"For God's sake, no! Just get her out of there!"

"Will you tell me one thing?" I asked. "Will you tell me who she is?"

There was a brief pause while he got hold of himself, and then very quietly he said, "Why do you want to concern yourself with this woman, Fred? She isn't a good type of woman, believe me."

"I'd prefer it," I said, "if you didn't call me Fred."

"She's cheap," he said. "She's uneducated. She's lower class. She's not your sort at all."

"What did she have to do with Uncle Matt?"

"Uhhhhhh. Well, she lived there."

"On Central Park South?"

"The doormen hated her."

"Wait a second. You mean, she lived with Uncle Matt."

"Your uncle was a different sort of man," he said. "Rough and ready, a sort of pioneer type. Not like you at all. Naturally, his taste in women differs from yours, and so the sort of woman he would—"

"Thank you," I said, and hung up.

She was seated on the sofa, legs crossed, one arm stretched out across the top of the sofa back. She was wearing black spike-heel shoes with straps halfway up the shin, nylons, a black skirt, and a white blouse with a frill at the throat. The blouse was coming out of the skirt at the side, revealing pale skin. She had also been wearing a black jacket, but that was now hanging on the doorknob.

She said, "So he gave you the word, did he?"

"He said I should get you out of here. I shouldn't listen to you. You're lower class."

"Is that right?" She bridled a bit, and said, "*He's* the one you shouldn't listen to, the shyster crook. He'd peddle his sister for candy bars and cheat her on the split."

That about summed up my own impression of Attorney Goodkind, but the fact that this woman—could she possibly be named Gertie Divine?—and I shared an enmity did not necessarily mean I could trust her. I said, "I suppose I might as well look at this letter."

"I suppose you might as well," she said. She picked it up from her lap and handed it to me. "While you're reading," she said, "how about a little hospitality?"

I didn't want to offer her a drink because I didn't want her to have an excuse to stay any longer than necessary, so I pretended not to have heard, turned my back, and opened the letter.

It was short, pungent, and difficult to read, being also in the same scrawled shaky masculine handwriting. It said:

Nepheu Fred,

This will interduce Gertie Divine, who used to headline at the Artillery Club in San Antonio. She has been my faithful companion and nurse, and she is the best thing I got to pass on to you. You keep her happy and I give you a garantee she'll keep you happy.

> Your long lost uncle,
> Matt

I looked up from the letter and found myself alone in the living room. Then I heard a clink of ice cubes, and went out to the kitchen to find Gertie Divine making a screwdriver with tomorrow morning's orange juice. "You want something, gracious host," she said to me, "you can make it yourself."

I held the letter up. I said, "What does this thing mean?"

"It means I'm yours now, honey," she said. She picked her drink up and went off the other way. "Is this the bedroom back here?"

Six

A few minutes after Gertie Divine went out to the supermarket there was a tentative tapping at my door, and when I opened it Wilkins from the second floor was there, lugging an ancient scuffed black suitcase all done up with broad leather straps. He set the suitcase down, puffed, shook his head, and said, "Not as young as I used to be."

There didn't seem to be anything to say to that. Besides, my head was still full of the problem of Gertie Divine, and what was I to do with her when she came back. If she came back. Anyway, I simply stood there and looked at Wilkins and his suitcase and continued to think about Miss Divine.

Wilkins was all in blue, as usual; one of his old Air Force blue shirts and a blue ink-stained right hand. After puffing a while longer and shaking his head some more, he finally said, "Like to see you, my boy. Like to take a minute of your time."

"Certainly, sir," I said, though I wasn't certain at all. "Come on in. Here, let me take that—"

But before I could get to the suitcase he'd swooped onto it himself, grasping its ancient handle and lifting it out of my

reach. "S'all right," he said hastily, like the hero of embezzle-
ment movies when a redcap has offered to carry the bag of
swag, "I'll take it myself."

In order to carry the suitcase at all, he had to lean far over
in the opposite direction, so that he stood like a number 7, in
which position he could just barely walk, clumping one foot
forward at a time and swiveling his whole body with each step.
Thus he came staggering into my apartment, looking as comic
and deformed as a Beckett hero.

In the center of the living room he finally set the suitcase
down again, and proceeded to puff some more. He also wiped
his hand across his forehead, using the ink-stained hand, leaving above his brows the cartoonist's triple streak representing
speed, so that he now reminded me of an ancient and wizened
Mercury.

Hospitality seemed required of me, I had no idea why, so
I said, "Uh, would you care for a drink?"

"Alcohol? No, no, thanks, I never touch alcohol. My late
wife broke me of the habit thirty-seven years ago. Thirty-eight,
come September. Wonderful woman."

"How about some coffee?"

He cocked a quizzical brow at me. "Tea?" he asked.

"Of course," I said. "No trouble. I'll just be a minute, take
a seat there."

I went to the kitchen to make the tea, and there I could
get back to my interior monologue about Gertie Divine. She
had apparently moved in, though not exactly with bag and baggage, and so far as I could tell she intended to stay here. What
she intended the arrangements to be I could only guess, but I
thought the guess a good one, and the prospect a bad one.

But what was I to do? She just *assumed* everything; she
marched cheerfully along without the faintest thought that
someone else might not agree with her plans. Like searching

my kitchen, announcing I had no food at all worthy of the name, and then snapping her fingers at me and saying, "Give me ten bucks, I'll go to the store."

Had I argued? Had I refused? Had I asked her who she thought she was? No. What I'd done was take out my wallet, give her the ten-dollar bill the bogus cop hadn't taken, and open the door for her when she left, patent-leather purse swinging from her forearm.

I had brave thoughts about refusing to let her in when she returned, I had bittersweet thoughts about her running off with my ten dollars and not returning at all, but in my heart I knew what was going to happen. She was going to come back with a double sack of groceries, she was going to order me to put them away while she ripped down the curtains in my living room, and I was going to put those awful groceries away.

Ah, well. In the meantime there was Wilkins. I made us both cups of tea, and when I brought them into the living room he was still standing beside his suitcase, exactly as I'd left him.

I said, "Why don't you sit down, sir?"

"Ah, tea!" he exclaimed, and took a cup from me, and stood there holding it, smiling brightly and falsely at me. "Heard about your good fortune," he said. "Want to offer my congratulations."

"You heard? How?"

"Phoned the authorities. What did you call it? Bunco Squad. Wondered how things had gone this morning."

"And they told you."

"Said I was neighbor, friend. Polite young man, most helpful."

"I see." I glanced at the suitcase. "And, uh, that?"

He looked down and smiled more broadly than ever, saying, "Life's work, my boy. Planned to show it you, never got around till now."

"Life's work? You mean, something to do with the Air Force?"

He smirked, and winked, and screwed his face up into remarkable expressions, and said archly, "You could say so, my boy, you could say so."

I had no idea what it was all about, and with my distraction over Gertie Divine, I really didn't care. I carried my cup of tea over to my reading chair and sat down. Wilkins could either take the hint and sit down himself or he could go on standing guard over the suitcase indefinitely, the choice was up to him.

Wilkins watched me avidly, waiting for me to express burning curiosity about his damn suitcase, but when it finally became obvious to him that no burning was about to begin he abruptly went over to the rocker, sat down, put his tea on the marble-top table to his left, and said, "Really a nice place you've got here. Fixed up first-rate."

"Thank you very much."

"So difficult to get just the right furnishings these days."

"Yes, it is," I said.

"'Specially on retired pay. Can't do much on short rations, can we?" He did a sort of barking laugh, picked up his teacup, and slurped down a huge swallow.

"It does take careful shopping," I said, wondering what on earth we were talking about and why we were talking about it. Meanwhile, in the middle of the room the suitcase had begun to grow. Not literally, of course, but in my mind. While Wilkins had been making such a fuss about it I couldn't have cared less about the thing, but now that we appeared to be talking about furniture or shopping or short rations or whatever it was, now that we weren't concerning ourselves with the suitcase at all, its enigmatic presence in the middle of the floor, all wrapped in leather straps with blackened buckles, was beginning to prey on my mind. What could be inside the thing, what could it contain? A model airplane? A set of spaceship plans? An H bomb?

"What a man really needs, these days," Wilkins was meanwhile saying, oblivious of my growing curiosity, "is a lot of money. Cash on the line. Of course, the best way to do it is your way, inherit the lot, don't lift a finger, let it fall your way. But those of us not so lucky, we've got to scrounge around, find a way to make ends meet and hope to build up for a windfall, something to put us on Easy Street."

Although this entire speech had been said in an open and friendly and chipper fashion, I suddenly found myself feeling guilty at having come so abruptly into unearned wealth. I said, "Well, I suppose it is difficult on a fixed income . . ."

"Not fixed for long," he announced, even more chipper than before. He nodded his head toward the huge suitcase. "That's what that's all about, of course. Make a killing."

"You said you wanted to show it to me," I said, as casually as possible, trying my best to cover my curiosity.

"Naturally," he said, beaming in a friendly fashion at me but not getting up from the rocker. "Any time at all. Any time you're free."

"Then there's no time like the present," I said. But an instant later I thought that had sounded too eager, and added, "If you don't have to hurry off anywhere, that is."

"Not at all, not at all. Happy to show you." Now at last he did get into motion, clinking the teacup back into its saucer, bounding to his feet, and dropping immediately to his knees in front of the suitcase. Wrestling the suitcase over onto its side and going to work undoing the leather straps, he said, "Young man like—you—be very interested I'm sure—. Thirty-one years—work here, thirty-one. Got it all worked—*there* it is!— all worked out."

With which he opened the top of the suitcase and looked

up at me like the genie delivering treasure to Aladdin.

Treasure? The suitcase was full of paper, typewriter paper, six stacks of it filling the interior. The top page of each stack—and, I suspected, all the pages underneath—was completely covered with writing in ink in a tiny but neat hand. The ink was the same shade of dark blue as Wilkins' right hand.

I said, "What is it?"

"My book," he said reverently. He patted the nearest stack of papers. "This is it."

"Your book?" A sort of dread overtook me, and I said, "You mean, your autobiography?"

"Oh, no! Not at all, no. I didn't have that sort of career, not me, no. Quiet tour, quiet tour." He gazed down fondly at his stacks of paper. "No, this isn't fact at all. But based on fact, naturally, based on fact."

"A novel, then," I said.

"In a way, in a certain way. But the history is accurate." He squinted at me as though to demonstrate how accurate he'd been, and said, "To the finest detail. Facts almost impossible to find, all in here, all accurate. Studied the era, got it all down."

Still groping in the dark, I said, "It's a historical novel."

"In a manner of speaking," he said. Kneeling there beside his suitcase full of paper, he leaned toward me, braced one hand on his manuscript, and whispered, "It's a retelling of the campaigns of Julius Caesar, with the addition of aircraft."

I said, "I beg your pardon?"

"I call it," he said, "*Veni, Vidi, Vici Through Air Power.* Pretty good, eh?"

"Pretty good," I said faintly.

He peered at me shrewdly, squinting only one eye. "You don't see it yet," he said. "You think the notion's a little loony."

"Well, it's just new," I said. "I'm not used to it yet."

"Of course it's new! That's half the point. What makes it to the big time, ever ask yourself?"

"I'm not sure," I said.

"Originals! It isn't the imitations that get on the best-seller list, it's the new ideas, the original thoughts. Like this!"

He thumped his manuscript for emphasis and we both looked with surprise at the sound of the thud. I said, "Well, it does sound original."

"Naturally it's original!" Now he was warmed to his task; crouched forward, hands gesturing, he explained it all to me. "I've kept the historical facts, kept them all. The names of the barbarian tribes, strength of armies, the actual battles, kept everything. All I've added is air power. Through a fluke of fate the Romans have aircraft, at about World War I level. So we see the sort of difference air power makes by putting it in a historical setting where it wasn't there."

I said, "You mean, how it changes history and all?"

"Well, it doesn't change history that much," he said. "After all, Caesar won almost all the battles he was in anyway. So not much is different afterwards. But the *battles* are different. And the psychology of the commanders is different. I've got it all down here, all down here. Julius, now, Julius Caesar himself, he's really something. Quite a character, quite a character. Wait till you read it."

"You want me to read it?" But that didn't sound right, so I immediately said, "I'll be glad to read it. I'd like very much to read it."

"It's an exciting idea, that's why," he told me. "You look at it right off the bat, you say to yourself, that's loony. Loony idea. But then it gets to you, you see how it has to be. Rickety little airplanes coming over the hills into Gaul, dropping spears and rocks—"

"They don't have guns?"

"Of course not. Gunpowder wasn't invented till a long time after that, long time. What I'm keeping here, I'm keeping accuracy. Aircraft is all they've got."

"But," I said, "if they have airplanes, that means they have the internal combustion engine. And gasoline. And refined oils. And if they've got all that, they'd just about have to have everything else, all the things we've got right now. Automobiles. Elevators. And bombs, too, maybe even atomic bombs."

"Don't worry about that," he said, smiling, sure of himself, and he patted his manuscript again. "It's all in here, all worked out in here."

I said, "Have you got a publisher?"

"Publisher!" Sudden rage flushed his face dark red, and his hands closed into fists. "Blind!" he shouted. "Every last one of them! Either they want to steal a man's work, or they don't see the potential. Potential, that's the word, and they don't see it. Stick with the tried and true, that's all they know. A man comes along with something really new, really different, really exciting, they don't know what to do with it."

"They've been rejecting it?"

"Went to one fellow," he said more quietly. "Said he'd publish it. Some sort of cooperation thing, I pay the expenses, printing costs and all that, he publishes it and sends the copies around to the bookstores. I don't know, I didn't think that was how they worked it, but he says so. Showed me a lot of books he published that way. Looked good, some of them, nice job, bright colors on the front, good paper, nice printing. Never heard of the books, though. That worries me. Of course, I'm not a reader, not that much, not outside my specialty. You, now, you probably heard of all of them. Some, anyway."

"I don't do much reading myself," I said. "Contemporary reading. Most of my reading is research."

"Like myself," he said happily. "Two of a kind, we are."
He smiled at me, then smiled at his manuscript. "Done now,"
he said.

"That's good," I said.

"Fellow said all the big names started out that way," he
said, gazing off into the middle distance. "Publishing their own
books, going in with fellows like him. D. H. Lawrence, he says.
James Joyce. All sorts of big names."

"It could be," I said. "I really don't know that much about
literary history."

"Naturally it costs a few thousand dollars," he said. "And
then more after that, for the publicity. You don't get anywhere
in this world today without publicity, believe you me. Got my
own ideas for publicizing this book. Ad copy to knock your eye
out, put it right in the *New York Times*. Papers all over the
country. Get the message across to the reading public."

"That sounds expensive," I said, feeling tremors of a pre-
monition.

"Takes money to make money," he said. "But think of the
profits. Book sales, that's only the beginning. Foreign publish-
ers. Movies, there's bound to be a movie in this. Got a suggested cast list here, Jack Lemmon for the young Julius Caesar,
Barbara Nichols—got it right . . ." He began rooting around
among the stacks of manuscript, without success, until he said,
"Oh, here's this. Cover. Rough idea."

He held toward me a sheet of paper containing a drawing
of sorts, also done in the inevitable dark-blue ink. Two lines of
lettering across the top, done shakily in a style reminiscent of
the Superman logo, read:

VENI, VIDI, VICI

THROUGH AIR POWER

"That's just a rough sketch," Wilkins told me unnecessarily. "I'm no artist. Have to hire someone to do it right."

He seemed to know his limitations; anyway, he was right about not being an artist. I couldn't for the life of me figure out what the drawing was supposed to be. It contained any number of lines, some straight and some curved, some long and some short, most crossing several others, but what they were supposed to represent I couldn't begin to guess. Could this possibly be a rickety biplane coming over the hills into Gaul? There was no way to tell. I very nearly turned the sheet upside down, to see if it made any more sense that way, but stopped myself in time, knowing it would surely insult Wilkins, who would think I'd done it deliberately to make fun of his drawing ability.

I said, "I don't seem to be able to—this doesn't—"

"It's Caesar and his staff," Wilkins explained, "standing beside one of the airplanes." He was still kneeling there, beside his suitcase, and now he clumped over to me on his knees and began pointing at various scrawls on the sheet, saying, "There's the plane," and, "There's Julius," and, "There's one of the loyal Goth commanders."

There was nothing to do but nod and say, "Yes, of course. Very nice." Which is what I did.

When we were done looking at the drawing, Wilkins took it back, clumped over to his suitcase again, and returned it to its spot somewhere in the middle of the manuscript. Doing so, not looking at me, he said, "What I need now, naturally, is financing. Split the profits fifty-fifty with the right man. Kindred spirit, money to invest. Fellow at the publishing house does the printing, distributing, simply for cash, no percentage of profits. I do the book, ad copy, all publicity, appearances, *Tonight Show*, et cetera, take fifty percent. Third fellow finances, gets it started, sits back, gets fifty percent."

I was beginning to feel very nervous. Wilkins was by no means a con man, he wasn't trying here to cheat me out of any money, but it was by now patently obvious he wanted me to invest in the publication of his novel, and I had no idea how I could possibly refuse him. What could I say? Any refusal at all would be an aspersion on the novel, and that would be insulting.

Actually I liked Wilkins, liked his ink-stained appearance, his offbeat way of speaking, his neat and mouselike air of self-containment. I didn't want to hurt his feelings, didn't want us avoiding each other's eyes during chance meetings by the mailbox.

Besides, what did I know about publishing, or novels? Though it did seem unlikely that Wilkins had actually written a bestseller, think how many bestsellers there have been that must have looked at least as unlikely beforehand. But the right people got behind them and pushed, the time was right, *something* was right, and there you are. And with publicity, a strong, well-financed ad campaign, Wilkins just might have something after all.

But I had to be sensible about it. After all, I had money now, a great deal of money, and if I was ever going to learn to be alert about money, this was the time. It was true that Wilkins wasn't a con man, but that didn't necessarily mean his novel wasn't a gold brick.

The thing for me to do, before even considering an investment, was talk to this publisher he had in mind, see what the man said, what he thought the prospects were. Always go to a specialist in the field, that's the rule.

I said, "Have you signed any contract with this publisher yet?"

"Well, it can't be done," he said, "without the guarantee of cash. Chap has his own expenses, after all, he can't just go around signing contracts with every crackpot walks into the office. A man has to show he's serious about it, has to put the money on the line."

"You're supposed to see him again, is that it?"

"We left it open," Wilkins said eagerly. "I'm to call if I get a fellow to go in with me."

"I suppose the thing to do—" I started, and there came a sudden loud knocking at the door. "One minute," I said to Wilkins, and went over and opened the door.

I'd completely forgotten about Gertie Divine, but in she came now with two sacks of groceries, just as I'd anticipated. "You owe me three bucks," she said, and came on into the living room, and looked with some surprise at Wilkins, kneeling there on the floor beside the open suitcase. "What's this?" she asked. "A prayer meeting?"

"My neighbor, Mr. Wilkins," I said. "Mr. Wilkins, this is, uh, Miss Divine. She was a friend of my uncle."

Still holding the sacks of groceries, she gazed down at Wilkins and said, "What's that you got there, Pop, the minutes of the last meeting?"

Wilkins abruptly shut the lid of the suitcase and said to me, "Can she be trusted?"

Gertie met his suspicion with an equal dose of her own. Turning around, peering at me from between the grocery bags, she said, "What's this geezer got in mind, Fred?"

Wilkins answered her, saying frostily, "Mr. Fitch and I are in partnership. It's a confidential matter at the moment."

"Oh, is it?"

I said, "Mr. Wilkins has written a novel—"

"And he wants it published," she finished. "And you're supposed to spring the geetus to some vanity house."

I blinked. "Vanity house?"

"When you write a stinking book and nobody wants it,"

she said, "you go to a vanity house and they soak you for whatever you got. I had a girlfriend once, she did this exposé, The Real True Life of a Stripper, called *The Shame of the Ecdysiast.* Cost her sixty-five hundred bucks to get the thing published, sold eight hundred copies, got one stinking review. And *they* hated it."

Frozen-voiced and frozen-faced, Wilkins said, "The gentleman I have been in contact with happens to be president of a respectable old-line firm, they publish a full line of—"

"Crap." She looked at me, made a motion of her head toward Wilkins, and said, "Throw the old bum out."

"Now, see here," said Wilkins, getting creakily up from his knees.

"Never mind," Gertie told me. "Just hold these." She dumped the two sacks in my arms, turned around, grasped Wilkins by the arm, and walked him briskly to the door. As he went by me I saw him looking absolutely blank with astonishment, an astonishment that kept him speechless until he was already out in the hallway, where he managed to wail, "My manuscript!"

"Coming up," Gertie told him. Back she came, gathered up the suitcase as though it were a six-pack of beer, carried it to the hallway, and heaved it out the door. I seemed to hear a repeated and receding series of thumps, as though something heavy were falling down stairs. I seemed also to hear a fluttering sound, as though from the beating of many tiny wings. I know I heard, before Gertie slammed the door, Wilkins give vent to a cry of despair.

I stood there knowing I should do something about this, stop Gertie, help Wilkins, assert myself, but all I did was stand there. And it wasn't simply cowardice, though that was a part of it. It was also relief, the knowledge that the decision about Wilkins' novel had been taken out of my hands. It wouldn't have been possible for me to say no to Wilkins, though in the back of my mind I had known all along I should say no to him, and it was with great relief and guilty pleasure that I permitted Gertie to wrest the decision out of my hands.

Gertie came back into the living room, brushing her hands and looking pleased with herself. She looked at me, stopped, put her hands on her hips, and said, "What are you doing, standing there? Put the goods away."

I said, plaintively, "You won't tear down my living-room curtains, will you?"

"Why the hell should I do something like that?"

"God alone knows," I said, and went off to the kitchen to put the groceries away.

SEVEN

What with one thing and another I'd completely forgotten Reilly's having told me about the visitors I would be getting from Homicide, so when someone knocked at my door at four o'clock my first impulse—since I believed it was probably Wilkins with a shotgun—was to ignore it.

Unfortunately—or maybe fortunately—my impulses no longer mattered around this place. As I sat there in the living room, trying to assemble the jigsaw puzzle of my mind, Gertie came striding through from the kitchen, carrying a sharp knife speckled with celery in her right hand, and opened the door before I could think of how to stop her.

God knows what the detectives thought, having the door opened to them by a woman with a knife in her hand. But they recognized her, so I suppose that cut short their shock. In any case, I heard a masculine voice say, "Well, if it isn't Gertie. You part of the inheritance, honey?"

"That's just what I am, Steve," she said. "You boys here on business?"

"Official is as official does," said the voice known as Steve.

"Then come on in," said Gertie, and stepped back to allow into my home two men who looked almost exactly like the phony cop who'd worked the counterfeit con on me this morning.

Gertie said to me, "Here's Steve and Ralph, a couple of dicks." Motioning at me, she told them, "That's Fred Fitch, Matt's nephew. I suppose he's the one you want to see."

"You're the one I want to see, Gertie," said Steve, as roguish as a bulldozer, "but Fred here is the one I want to talk to."

"I got dinner on," she said. "You boys will excuse me."

"For almost anything, Gertie," said Steve, laying his gallantry on with a trowel.

She gave him an arch grin and walked out, and Steve turned to me, his manner suddenly becoming Prussian. He said, "You are Fredric Fitch?"

"That's right," I said. I got to my feet and said, "Would you like to sit down?"

They promptly sat down, the both of them, and then I sat down again and began to feel very foolish. I said, "Uh, Jack Reilly told me you'd be coming to see me."

"We got a report," Steve told me. "As we understand it, you didn't know about this bequest you got until today, is that it?"

"That's right," I said. "Well, no, not exactly. I heard about it yesterday, but I didn't believe it until today."

"That's kind of a shame," Steve said, straight-faced. "Knocks you out of being our number-one suspect."

Ralph, speaking for the first time, explained, "You see, you've got the best motive we know about."

"*Only* motive we know about," said Steve.

"So naturally," said Ralph, "we're disappointed about you not knowing about the inheritance in advance."

"And naturally," said Steve, "we'd like to bust that story if we could, because then we could have our number-one suspect back."

Feeling the faint flutter of butterfly wings in my belly, I said, "You don't really suspect me, do you?"

"Well, that's just it," said Steve. "We can't, can we?"

"It's not having the choice," Ralph explained, "that's what bothers us so."

"And of course," said Steve, "there are what you might call weird elements to the case."

"Which we don't like either," said Ralph.

"Weird elements make us nervous," said Steve.

I said, "I don't know what you mean, weird elements."

Steve said, "According to our information, you never met your Uncle Matt, is that right?"

"That's right."

"Never even heard of him, in fact."

"That's right."

"Yet he left you almost half a million bucks."

"Three hundred thousand," I corrected.

"Before taxes," he said. "Half a million before taxes."

"Yes."

"To a nephew he'd never met, a nephew that didn't even know he existed."

"That's right," I said.

"That strikes us," Ralph explained, "as a weird element."

"Then there's this business about not telling you about the inheritance until a couple weeks after the old guy's dead. Right in the will it says this." Steve spread his hands. "That's also what we like to call between ourselves a weird element."

"Not to mention Gertie," said Ralph.

"Exactly," said Steve. "Here you have this old guy dying

of cancer, he's got about as much get up and go as a wet noodle, and yet he—"

I said, "Dying?"

"Isn't that something?" said Ralph. "One foot in the grave already and the proverbial other one on a banana peel, and somebody has to hurry him along."

"I didn't know about that," I said.

"So that's another element of the sort we call a weird element," said Steve. "Bumping a guy going in a day or two anyway. Not to mention Gertie, like Ralph said."

I said, "Was he really that close to death? A day or two?"

"He's been that close the last five years," Ralph told me. "That's what his doctor says. He was down in Brazil, Matt Grierson was, and he found out he had cancer, and he came home to die."

"Not to mention Gertie," said Steve. "Except I think maybe it's time we did mention Gertie."

I said, "What about her?"

"That's what your uncle picks for a nurse," said Steve. "Gertie Divine, the Body Secular."

"Was she really a stripper?" I asked.

Steve was surprised at me. "Certainly," he said. "I seen her myself, over in Passaic, not so many years ago. And you ask me, she's still got the old pizzazz."

Ralph said, "Steve's had the hots for Gertie ever since we come on this case."

"Longer," Steve said. "Since Passaic. But anyway, that isn't the point. The point is a terminal cancer patient, what the doctors call a terminal cancer patient, and an old bozo to boot, that's what he picks for his nurse. Then he gets bumped and his nephew gets all his loot, and when we come around for a nice talk with the nephew, who's here? Gertie. There's another weird element, what we think of around the station house as a weird element."

Ralph said, "How long have you known Gertie, Fred?"

I wanted to call him Ralph, I really wanted to call him Ralph. I wanted to start my answer with Ralph and end my answer with Ralph and put Ralphs in here and there in the middle of the answer, and answer only in words which were anagrams of Ralph. But I'm a coward. I didn't even call him Ralph once. I said, "I just met her today. She was here when I came back from the lawyer's."

They blinked at me, in unison. Steve said, "You mean, she just walked in? Cold?"

"Not cold, Steve," said Ralph.

"All right," conceded Steve, "not cold. But just walked in. You never saw her before."

"Let me show you something," I said, and got to my feet.

"I'd be delighted to see it," said Steve. "We both would."

"Delighted," said Ralph.

I went over to the desk and took Uncle Matt's letter of introduction out of the pigeonhole I'd filed it in, and brought it to Steve, and handed it to him. He read it, and grinned, and said, "Now, isn't that something new." He handed the letter to Ralph. "Here's something entirely different, Ralph," he said.

Ralph read the letter. When he was done he said, "There's a thing I notice about this letter."

Steve said, "What's that, Ralph?"

"It doesn't seem to have a date on it," said Ralph.

"She just brought it here today," I said, somewhat defensively.

"I accept that," said Ralph. "What I wonder about, I wonder when he wrote it. You follow me?"

"Why don't we ask her?" I said.

Steve said, "I don't think that'll be necessary, Fred. Do you, Ralph?"

"Not at the moment," said Ralph.

With me standing up and then sitting down I felt better than before, and more sure of myself. I said, "If my uncle was dying anyway, and if he was hit with a blunt instrument, isn't it likely he was killed in a quarrel with somebody? Some sort of rage, no real motive at all."

"It is a possibility," said Steve. "I certainly do go along with you on that, Fred, what you bring up there is a possibility. And I believe we're doing some work along those lines already. Aren't we, Ralph?"

"Routine work along those lines," said Ralph. "That's what we're doing, yes."

"Of course, at the same time," said Steve, "I admit to you in all frankness and honesty I wouldn't mind turning up with somebody saw you and your Uncle Matt together six months ago. Or you and Gertie. Right, Ralph?"

"Help us considerably," said Ralph.

"I'm sorry," I said, "but I'm telling the truth."

"Oh, I don't doubt it," Steve said fatalistically. "But a fella can dream, can't he?"

Ralph said, "You wouldn't have anything you might want to tell us that we don't already know, would you?"

"About the murder?"

"That's the case we're working on, yes."

"I never heard about it myself till this afternoon, I don't know a thing about it. Only what Reilly told me and what you told me."

"And what Gertie told you."

"Gertie doesn't tell me a thing. At least, she hasn't yet."

Steve laughed. "A good old girl, Gertie," he said. He heaved to his feet, looking very strong and tough. "Don't let me hear about you giving her a bad time, Fred," he half-joked.

"I don't think that's the way it'll go," I said.

Ralph also stood up. "I guess we'll be going along," he said. "Any time you want to get in touch with us, call Homicide South. Or try through your friend Reilly."

"I will," I said. "If I have any reason to call."

"That's right," said Ralph.

As they headed for the door, Steve said, "Tell Gertie so long for us, Fred. Tell her she's still my girl."

"I'll do that," I said, and stood fidgeting from one foot to the other until they finally left.

The slamming of the door brought Gertie out of the kitchen, looking around, saying, "They're gone?"

"Steve said to tell you so long."

"Cops are bums," she said philosophically. Then she frowned at me, saying, "Sweetie, this place is a mausoleum. Haven't you got a record player?"

"I doubt you'll care much for my records," I said.

"Honey, I figured that out already, but like the fella says, music is better than no music at all. Put on some of your string quartets, will you?"

I put on Beethoven's Ninth, full volume. If it was rock and roll she wanted, it was rock and roll she was going to get.

EIGHT

The next few hours were for me a time of muted panic. How totally Gertie had made herself at home! All I could think about was bed, and what she thought the sleeping arrangements were going to be. Though I did not consider myself a prude, and though technically I was not a virgin (I mean my abstinence had now lasted so long I could be thought of as having returned, at least honorarily, to virginal status), the notion of casually hopping into the sack with a stripper from the Artillery Club within a few hours of first meeting her—or even within a few months of first meeting her, to be honest—was paralyzing. On the other hand, to refuse any woman, much less a woman with the blunt strength of Gertie, is an extremely delicate operation at which I have not had a whole heck of a lot of practice.

Not that Gertie's presence was all bad, not by a long shot. She'd saved me from Wilkins, for instance, and the more I thought about that episode the more it seemed to me I had been in the process of being conned after all, via remote control, by the fellow who had offered to publish Wilkins' book for him at a price.

Besides that, Gertie turned out to have a really unexpected genius at cookery, producing a dinner the like of which I hadn't eaten for years, if ever. The basic ingredients were steak and potatoes and broccoli and salad, but the extras turned these basics into so many variations on manna. I ate myself round-faced.

During dinner, to make conversation and thus to distract myself from my panic, I asked Gertie what she thought about Uncle Matt having been murdered, and if she had any idea who might have done it.

"Not a one," she said. "Nobody saw nobody, nobody heard a thing. I wasn't home when it happened and nobody else was around."

I said, "It's been almost two weeks. I guess the police must be stuck."

"Cops," she said, in offhand contempt, and shrugged her shoulders, as though to say, What do you expect?

I felt as though I should take some sort of interest in Uncle Matt's death, since he *had* given me over three hundred thousand dollars, but it was hard to concentrate with Gertie over there carving away on her steak with such gusto. Nevertheless, I managed to keep on the track, saying, "Do you suppose it might have been someone he swindled? You know, getting revenge."

"Matt was retired for years," she said, and filled her mouth with salad.

"Well, out of the past," I said. "Someone who finally caught up with him."

She held up a hand for me to wait, sat there chewing salad, swallowed, put the hand down again, and said, "You mean a mark? From like twenty years back?"

"Maybe," I said.

"Forget it, honey," she said. "If a sucker catches on while he's still in the store he might take a poke at you, but not later on. That's the thing about suckers, they're *suckers.* They just go home and feel sorry for themselves, they don't go around tracking people down and bumping them off."

I felt my face getting red. She had described me so accurately that the next time I brought a forkful of potatoes up to my mouth I stuck the tines into my upper lip.

Meanwhile, Gertie was going on in a reminiscing sort of way, saying, "That's what Professor Kilroy used to say all the time, 'A sucker is a sucker.' It was like a philosophy with him."

"Professor who?"

"Professor Kilroy. Him and Matt was partners for years."

"Where's he these days?"

She shrugged. "Beats me. Prob'ly still in Brazil. What's the matter, you don't like your food?"

I had put my fork down. "I'm full," I said. "It was delicious, but I'm full."

"What an appetite," she said in disgust. "Why'd I waste my time?"

We finished the meal with nectar reminiscent of coffee, and then I staggered to my reading chair in the living room, where I lolled for the next hour, digesting and trying not to think about the events yet to come tonight and holding this morning's *Times* in front of my face upside down.

Until, at about seven-fifteen, Gertie appeared before me with her black jacket on and her patent-leather purse dangling from her left forearm. "Put yourself out a little," she said. "Walk me to the subway."

I looked up uncertainly and said, "Where are you going?"

"Home," she announced. "You think I got nothing better to do than hang around here all the time?"

A feeling of such relief washed over me then that I very nearly tossed my *Times* into the air and shouted whoopee, refraining only for fear it might hurt her feelings. But to know that Gertie was leaving, that she considered somewhere other than this place home, that she did not intend to remain here permanently like Bartleby, there was good news indeed.

Smiling, I said, "I'll be glad to walk you, Gertie." I folded the newspaper, got out of the chair, put my jacket on, and we left the apartment.

I felt strangely comfortable walking along the sidewalk with Gertie, felt none of the embarrassment I'd anticipated on the way downstairs. We walked to Eighth Avenue in companionable silence, and up to 23rd Street, where the subway entrance was and where it belatedly occurred to me—as I may have mentioned before, the word *belatedly* is my capsule autobiography—to offer Gertie money for a cab instead.

She instantly overreacted. Putting her hand to her heart—a not easy thing for Gertie to do—she pretended to be on the verge of a faint, and cried, "Oh, the spendthrift! He throws it around like it was pianos."

I knew how to handle Gertie now, so I said, "Of course, if you'd feel more at home in the subway—"

Her answer was to put two fingers in her mouth and give a whistle that shattered windows as far away as the UN Building. A cab yanked itself out of traffic and stopped, panting, at our feet.

I handed Gertie a dollar, at which she looked as though she'd never seen anything so small before. Then she said, in weary disgust, "A Hundred-twelfth Street, big spender."

In some confusion, I handed her another dollar, saying, "Is that enough?"

"No more," she said. "You'll spoil me."

I held the cab door for her, and after she got in I said through the window, "When will I see you again?" More in trepidation than anything else.

"Never," she said. "Unless you get my phone number."

"Oh," I said, and patted myself all over for paper and pencil, finding neither. (I rarely carry pen or pencil, as it makes it too easy for me to sign things.)

Finally the cab driver, who was probably Gertie's brother, or at least her cousin, leaned toward me with a filthy pencil stub and a gum wrapper in his outstretched hand, saying, "Here you go, Casanova."

I smoothed the gum wrapper out on the cab roof, and copied down Gertie's number as she reeled it off to me with all the care of instructions being given to a retarded child: "University five—that's U N, you know—University five nine nine seven oh. You got it?"

She wouldn't take my word for it, but made me read it back to her. Then I put it in my wallet, stepped back up onto the sidewalk, and the cab driver called to me, "Hey, Willie Sutton!"

I bent and squinted at him. "Eh?"

"The pencil," he said.

So I took his pencil out of my pocket and gave it to him and at last they raced away uptown. I could—although I didn't want to—imagine the conversation between them as they traveled, and my ears burned in sympathy.

And what was this other feeling? Jealousy? Jealous of Gertie Divine (the Body Secular, let's not forget that) and a cab driver? I felt like taking out my wallet again and checking to see who I was.

That's why I was so distracted as I walked back home, and why I paid no attention to the things around me. I was thinking about Gertie, whose phone number was unexpectedly in my wallet, and I was wondering what I was going to do about that phone number in future.

I had been far from tranquil about the apparent arrangements up till Gertie's abrupt departure, but one thing could be said in their favor: I wasn't in charge. Whatever was happening or going to happen was completely out of my hands, which can be a really liberating feeling, particularly for a tongue-tied recluse.

But now all that had been changed. All at once everything was up to me. I had no doubt Gertie would never re-enter my life without a specific invitation from me, and that fact left me hip-deep in a quandary. Did I *want* to call her? And if I did, what on earth for?

These questions took about ninety-five percent of my attention, leaving very little for the world around me. I did hear the backfire as I crossed 21st Street, but paid it no mind. And I heard the second backfire as I turned into 19th Street, almost simultaneous with the sound of someone breaking glass nearby, but ignored that one as well.

The third backfire should have made more impression than it did, particularly since it was immediately followed by a *brrrringgg* sound from a trash can in front of the building I was passing, but I paid it no more attention than the others, and so I was totally unprepared when a street urchin of about twelve came up to me, tugged at my sleeve, and said, "Say, mister. That car just took a shot at you."

I looked at him, my mind still full of Gertie. "What's that?"

"That car," he said, pointing down the street. "They just took a shot at you."

Assuming I was being kidded, I said, "Of course. Very funny."

"You think I'm lying? Take a look at the garbage can there."

Was he serious? I said, "Why?"

"'Cause that's what they plugged," he said. "Take a look at the hole."

Suddenly I remembered the backfires, the sound of glass breaking, the ringing of the trash can. The boy was right, somebody was shooting at me!

While I was gaping at him, trying to encompass this incredible idea, he pointed down the street behind me and said, "Here they come again."

"What? Who?"

"C'mere," he said urgently, grabbed my sleeve, and the two of us ducked into a cellar entranceway. "Keep cool," the boy advised me. "They didn't see us come in here."

I tried to see what was happening out in the street, but it was difficult while at the same time trying to keep from being seen. Also, the street was lined with parked cars. Nevertheless, I did see the black car go slowly by, as ominous as the silence in the middle of a storm. I couldn't see who was driving or how many people were in the car, but it seemed to me the aura of menace around it was inescapable.

After they'd gone the boy said, "You want me to go get a cop?"

"No, that's all right," I said. "I live just a few doors from here." I got out my wallet, fished a bill from it without exactly knowing its denomination—I only knew it had to be either a single or a five—and in some embarrassment pressed it into the boy's hand, saying, "A small token of my esteem."

He took it casually and said, "Sure. They tryna keep you from testifying?"

"I don't think so," I said. "I'm not sure what they're doing."

"They're shooting at you," he said reasonably.

"Yes. Well, goodbye."

"See you around," he said.

I took the remaining half-block to my building at a dead run, went up the stairs to the third floor at the same breakneck speed, and stopped short at my door with the sudden thought: *What if they're in there!*

I stood indecisively in the hallway a minute or two, trying to think of some way to test for the presence of assassins in my apartment, but ultimately decided there was no way to test other than actually entering the apartment and seeing what happened. What finally emboldened me to do so was the thought that if they—whoever they were—had access to my apartment it was unlikely they would be driving around the city taking potshots at me from moving cars.

My supposition was correct; the apartment was as empty as I'd left it. After a quick search of all the rooms and all the closets I got on the phone and called Reilly at home, but he wasn't there. So I tried him at Headquarters and he wasn't there either.

Now what? I wanted to report this to the police, of course, but on the other hand I felt a little foolish just calling up some strange policeman and saying, "Someone is shooting at me from a car." It would require so much explanation, and in fact, most of the explanation I wouldn't even be able to offer.

I thought of phoning Steve and Ralph, the Homicide detectives—it seemed to me very likely that the people shooting at me were the same ones who had killed my Uncle Matt—but there was just something so oppressive about that vaudeville team that I doubt I would have phoned them if there'd been an assassin in every closet in the place.

No, what I wanted was my friend Reilly. Let *him* tell the other police. I called him again at home, hoping against hope, but there was still no answer, so I returned disconsolately to my reading chair, sat down in it, and failed to read the *Times*.

Every five minutes between then and eight-thirty I tried Reilly again, and never did find him home. Then, at eight-thirty, I remembered the girl who had approached me in Madison Square Park, the one who had warned me I was in danger and claimed to be on my side. I hadn't believed her on either count at the time, but now it seemed that at least the first half of her statement was true. If people were shooting at me, it seemed fair to say that I was in danger.

Could the second half also be true? Was it possible she *was* on my side? Was it possible she could tell me who was shooting at me and why?

Nine o'clock, she'd said, that was when I was supposed to meet her at her place tonight—160 West 78th, I'd remembered the address without wanting to.

Should I go? It would mean leaving here now, because to get there later than nine o'clock might be useless. But I hated to go up there alone, without Reilly, without at least talking it over with Reilly, telling him what had happened and asking him what he thought we should do about it.

I'll give him one last chance, I thought. I'll call him at home, and if he's there I'll tell him the whole story. But if he isn't there I'll go up to 78th Street myself and find out what's going on. Anything is better than just sitting here, twiddling my thumbs.

Naturally enough, he wasn't home.

Fine. Having made my decision, I was left with one other small problem; namely, how to leave this building and this neighborhood without being shot at anymore. After all, they couldn't reasonably be expected to go on missing forever.

Disguise myself? No. There were a total of three tenants in this building, and any watcher would readily guess who I had to be no matter what disguise I chose for myself.

Just bolt out the door and down the street, pell-mell? No again. A car can outrun a man every time. And if I were to betray the fact that I was now aware of them, they would throw aside subterfuge and attack much more openly.

The back way? There was a small garden behind the building, Mr. Grant's domain, enclosed by high fencing on three sides. I wasn't entirely sure, but it seemed to me that if one could get over that fence at the rear, it should be possible to get through the building behind this one and thus out onto the street one block away.

At any rate, it was worth a try. I changed to my black suit, put a dark sweater on under the jacket, and went downstairs to knock on Mr. Grant's door.

Didn't he ever do anything but eat? This time he had a chicken leg in his hand, as well as the inevitable napkin tucked into his collar. I said, "I'm sorry to interrupt you again, but I wonder if I could go out your back door."

He was so bewildered I felt sorry for him. He said, "My back door?" He turned around, as though looking for it.

"It would take too long to explain," I said. "It really would. But if you'd just let me go through your apartment and out the back door . . ."

"You mean, into my garden?"

"Well, through your garden. I want to go over the fence and into the building across the way."

"Across the way?"

"I promise to explain the first chance I get," I said.

I think he only stepped to one side, allowing me to enter, because it was easier than trying to understand me. He shut the door, then preceded me through his neat apartment to the rear door, unlocked and opened it, and stood aside again to let me out. As I stepped through he said, "You won't be coming back?"

"Not this way," I said. Which shows how little we know our own futures.

NINE

There was more than enough light, spilling from windows on all sides. I traversed the winding slate walk to the board fence at the far end of the garden, climbed up on a steel lawn chair there, hoisted myself the rest of the way up, and slid down the other side into a million rusting metal coils. Springs of some sort they were, attaching themselves to my feet or bounding off with mighty *sprongs* or merely clustering under me as I tried to regain my balance. There was nothing for it but that I should fall over, and so I did, with a crash and a clatter and a bi-di-*ding*.

I lay there unmoving, waiting for silence, which eventually arrived, to be immediately followed by the sound of a window being hurled open. A hoarse male voice shouted, "Shoo! Damn it, you cats shoo the hell out of there!"

I didn't move.

We both waited and listened for half a minute or so, and then he gave vent to a couple more half-hearted shoos and shut his window again.

It was impossible to move without sound effects. *Boing*

under my left knee, *greeek* under my chest, *chinkle* in the vicinity of my right arm. With many a *plink* and *tunkle* I crawled away from the fence and the ubiquitous springs, until I was at last clear of all of them except those which had attached themselves to my belt and cuffs. These I removed, with muffled *brangs*, and got rather shakily to my feet.

I was in a much darker yard than Mr. Grant's, and one not nearly so well kept. Directly in front of me was the building I was headed for, with a barred window and a shut door at ground-level. Though lights were on in the upper windows, the ground floor was in total darkness.

It hadn't occurred to me before that I would probably have to go through an apartment in this building, that the physical setup would more than likely be similar to my own building, with the rear entrance only to a ground-floor apartment. But I was apparently in luck; from the absence of light, and the time only a little past eight-thirty, it seemed this apartment must be empty.

I had never burgled a door before, and wasn't entirely sure how to go about it. I began with this one by rattling the knob and proving to my own satisfaction that it was, like every other door in New York City, locked.

But then I noticed that one of the panes of glass in the door was broken, replaced—temporarily, I suppose—by a piece of cardboard. How securely could a piece of cardboard be fastened? I pushed on it experimentally, and it gave, being attached on the inside only by masking tape. I pushed it farther open, reached in, opened the door from the inside, and stepped cautiously into pitch blackness.

My only guide was the faint gray rectangle of the window. If I kept that always behind me, and if I moved with extreme care, it seemed to me I must sooner or later navigate the entire apartment and emerge at the front of the building. Slowly, therefore, I began to shuffle forward.

I had shuffled about six shuffles when I heard a creak. I stopped. I listened.

A light went on. Bedside lamp, directly ahead of me ten feet or so. Hand still touching the lamp switch, long bare arm leading my eye to the right, where a naked woman was sitting up in a double bed, staring at me with the blank stunned gaze of someone awakened by the incomprehensible. Beside her, farther from the lamp, the mound of a second person, still asleep.

But not for long. Neither taking her hand from the lamp nor her eyes from me, the woman began to pummel the mound with her other fist, crying, "George! George, wake up! A prowler, George!"

I was frozen. I was incapable of movement or speech, and so could neither escape nor explain. I just stood there, like Lot's wife.

The mound abruptly sat up, proving to be a man with a remarkably heavy jaw and a remarkably hairy chest. He didn't look at me at all. Instead, he looked at the woman and said, slowly and dangerously, "Who's this George?"

She looked at him. She blinked. She put her hands to her face. She said, "Oh, my God, it's Frank!"

I didn't wait for any more, since I'd suddenly found my feet capable once again of motion. To the right of the bed was a doorway. I ran to it and full tilt into a closet full of female clothing.

I backed out again, sputtering and beating off dresses, and found Frank gradually becoming aware of my presence, if not my identity. He looked at me, staggering past with a white blouse wrapped around my neck, and said, "George? This is George?"

My only chance was out the door I'd come in. Flinging the

blouse at Frank, I spun out the door, across the yard in the direction of the fence and home, and back again into the Sargasso Sea of rusty springs. I flailed through these, and back there somewhere that window was flung up again and the hoarse male voice bellowed, "All right, cats, you asked for it!"

I attained the fence, but could do no more. I sagged against it, waiting for whatever was going to happen next. Behind me, in the doorway of the apartment I'd just left, Frank was standing buck-naked and shouting, "Come back here, George! Come back and fight like a man!" Meanwhile, the woman was tugging at him from behind and crying, "Frank, it's all a mistake, let me explain, Frank, please!"

Now another female voice suddenly cried, "Harry, you'll get the cops on us!"

The hoarse male voice roared, "Outa the way, Mabel, this time they're gonna get it!"

"Harry, don't!"

"Frank, please!"

"George, you bastard!"

From somewhere back there, something made a small sound. It sounded like pah. Near me a piece of metal went *ting*.

It happened again. First pah behind me, and then *ting* close by. And a third time. And a fourth time.

Pah-*ting*.

Pah-*ting*.

I didn't get it until there was a pah, and instead of a *ting* there was a sudden burning sensation in my right leg, just above the knee, as though I'd been stung by a wasp. Then I realized what was happening.

Harry was shooting at me with a BB gun.

Pah-*ting*.

I suddenly found new reserves of strength. Up and over the

fence I went, clawing my way, and collapsed in a heap across the lawn chair on the other side.

After a minute or two I had my wind back sufficiently to get to my feet, remove the springs that had attached themselves to my clothing, toss them back over the fence—which set off a new paroxysm of fury back there—and limp on down the path to Mr. Grant's back door.

I knocked, and soon he opened the door an inch, looked at me with some astonishment, and said, "Are you coming back?"

"Change of plans," I panted.

He looked past me, in the direction of all the noise. Over there beyond his fence it sounded as though a war were going on: shouts and shrieks and clamoring. Mr. Grant said, mildly, "What on earth is all that?"

"Some sort of wild party," I said. "Nothing to do with us." I slipped past him into the apartment. "Thank you very much," I said. "I'll be going now."

When I left him, he was a very baffled man.

TEN

There was a black car double-parked across the street, its motor throbbing. I stood in the vestibule, in darkness, and watched it for a while without seeing it do anything but sit there and throb. A liveried chauffeur sat in semidarkness behind the wheel, and black side curtains were drawn to hide the rear seat.

It was them, there was no question of it. They didn't know I'd finally become aware of them shooting at me before—or, that is, I'd finally been warned by a passing child—so they were waiting as bold as brass right in front of my door, expecting me sooner or later to come blithely out and down the steps and directly into a hail of gunfire.

Not a bit of it. I had to get out of here, and I was resigned to going out the front way, but something had to be done about that hail of gunfire.

I had one advantage. They didn't know that I knew that they were trying to kill me. With a little luck, plus the element of surprise, I might be able to get past them after all. Zip out the door, leap down the steps, race away along the sidewalk, be gone before they knew what was happening.

It sounded good, all right, but somehow I just wasn't doing it. Seconds ticked away forever, and I continued to lurk in the vestibule.

Until, looking far down the street to the right, I saw a police car coming, meandering along slowly the way they do, and I knew I was saved. They wouldn't dare shoot at me with a police car right next to them.

I tensed, I crouched, I closed my hand on the doorknob, I waited while the police car inched its way down the street and every nerve in my body slowly tied itself into a half-hitch. Until, until . . .

The police car approached the double-parked black automobile, started past it, came even with it . . .

And out the door I went, zip, according to plan. Down the steps, leap, and away along the sidewalk, race, and not a single shot was fired.

Also, it was a one-way street. They couldn't merely U-turn and come swooping after me, they would have to completely circle the block. With any luck, I could be in a cab and racing uptown long before they made it.

Of course, there's no such thing as a taxicab in New York City when you want one. That is, there are cabs, thousands and thousands of cabs, but they're all off-duty. They streamed by me in schools, in coveys, in congeries, every bloody one of them off-duty, while I waved my arms around like the signal-giver on an aircraft carrier.

At last there showed up a cab whose driver had apparently decided to work a second hour today. Into it I leaped, shouting, "Uptown! Hurry!" So up he dawdled to the next corner, where the light was red, and stopped there.

"These lights are set at twenty-two miles an hour, my friend," he said. "So that's the speed I'll hurry at, if it's okay with you."

"Whatever you say," I said, while simultaneously trying to hide myself from the world and look all around for the black car. I failed to see it, and I hoped it was failing to see me, and several weeks later the light changed and we began to crawl uptown at twenty-two miles an hour.

I was encouraged to see, when we turned onto 78th Street, that the only car that made the turn after us was a little gray Peugeot, driven by a woman in a huge floppy hat. As the Peugeot went on by us I paid the driver, left his cab, and hurried across the sidewalk and into the building.

Locked glass doors were in front of me, with a panel on the wall to their right containing nameplates and doorbells. But what was the name the girl had given me? I couldn't for the life of me remember.

Maybe if I looked at all the names, the right one would ring a bell. I ran my finger down the rows, looking at all the names . . .

Smith?

Could it possibly have been Smith? Surely no one would use the name Smith in a situation like this. And yet that was the only one that caught my attention at all. And it did seem as though I remembered her having used that name, giving me this address and then the name Smith.

Well. Obviously there was nothing to do but try. It was already ten minutes past nine, and getting later every second.

I pressed the button beside "Smith 3-B," and after a minute a metallic and vaguely female voice said through the grill above the nameplates, "Who is it?"

"Fitch," I told the grill. "Fred Fitch."

The door buzzed. I pushed it open and went into a long thirtyish lobby with the elevator at the far end.

The elevator was also on the ninth floor. I pushed the button and watched the numbers over the doors light slowly one after the other in reverse order. A while after the number 1 went on, the doors slid open and there was the elevator.

Apartment 3-B was to my right when I got off the elevator on the third floor. I rang its bell and the door immediately opened and standing there was the girl from Madison Square Park, wearing red canvas slacks and a sleeveless blouse in a kaleidoscope design. She was barefoot, and a highball glass in her right hand tinkled its ice at me.

"You're ten minutes late," she said.

"I had a little trouble," I said.

"Well, you're here," she said, "and that's the important thing. Come on in."

I entered a white hall, at the end of which I could see a portion of the living room. Miss Smith closed the door and said, "You're worth fifty bucks to me, do you know that?"

"What?"

"Come on along," she said, and preceded me along the carpeted hall to the living room.

There was nothing to do but follow. As she entered the living room she said to someone out of sight, "Okay, smart boy, pay up. You lose."

Something was wrong. I stepped hesitantly into the living room, ready to flee.

But it wouldn't do any good to flee. Reilly heaved his big frame up out of the sofa, put his drink down on the coffee table, and said to me in great disgust, "Okay, you silly bastard, explain yourself."

ELEVEN

Explain myself, he said. Well, he also had some explaining to do, and so for a while the apartment was knee-deep in explanations, as I described to them my having been shot at and they told me what they'd had in mind in inveigling me up here.

It seems Miss Smith, whose first name was Karen, was a friend of Reilly's, and he'd put her up to this. They had been talking about me—my ears burned at the idea—and it had been Reilly's contention that the windfall I had just received would make me, at long last, cautious in my dealings with strangers. Karen Smith had insisted she could work her wiles on me, inheritance or no inheritance. Reilly had said that if she could do it—that is, if I was still the same incorrigible sucker I'd always been—he wanted to know about it. If Karen could talk me into coming to this apartment tonight, without telling me any truth other than her last name and address, Reilly would owe her fifty dollars. If she failed, she owed Reilly fifty dollars.

I believed them about this harebrained bet, because that's the sort of plot that just naturally springs up around me, but Reilly for a long time wouldn't believe me about the shooting.

When finally he did come grudgingly around to accept it, he wanted to know why I hadn't reported it to the police. "I'm not the only cop in the world, you know," he said.

"You're the only cop in the world I know," I reminded him. "And I kept calling you, but you weren't home."

"So you thought you'd come up here."

"Well, Miss Smith had said—"

"Karen," she said, and smiled at me.

I smiled back at her. "Karen," I agreed. To Reilly I said, "She'd talked in the park there as though my life was in danger and she knew what it was all about. So I thought I'd come up and find out."

He sighed heavily and shook his head. "Let me give you a for instance, Fred. For instance, Karen is a gun moll in cahoots with the people that shot at you. So you come up here, and *they're* here."

"Well," I said. I looked helplessly at Karen. "I didn't think it could be like that," I said. "You just weren't that kind of girl."

She laughed and said, "Thank you, Mr. Fitch, thank you very much."

"Fred," I said.

"Fred," she agreed.

Reilly said, "Fred, that's just the kind of thing always gets you in trouble. When will you get it through your head that people aren't what they look like?"

"Sometimes they are," I said.

"Which times?"

I didn't have an answer, and Reilly was a little mad at me— the fifty dollars he owed Karen had something to do with that, I believe—so the conversation stalled there for a minute, with everybody looking at nobody, until Karen said brightly, "Let me get drinks for everybody. Fred?"

"Oh, Scotch, I suppose."

"Ice?"

"Please."

While she was away in the kitchen rattling ice-cube trays, Reilly said to me, "I don't suppose you got the kid's name."

I had no idea what he meant, and so said, "Who?"

"The kid," he said, not very patiently. "The one told you you'd been shot at."

"Oh. No, he didn't tell me. He was just a boy, one of the boys from the neighborhood."

He sighed again, "Fred," he said softly, "may I tell you how you should have handled this?"

"I wish you would."

"Then I will. You should have collared the kid and taken him straight to a phone and called your local precinct. The kid might have been able to describe the car. He might even have seen the people inside it."

"I don't think so," I said.

"You don't think so. In any case he was your witness. So you call the precinct, and when the officers arrive you tell them, "This kid says somebody was shooting at me.' It's simple."

"It sounds simple," I admitted, "the way you say it. But I don't know, it just didn't seem to work out that way."

"It never does, with you," he said. He sighed, and shook his head, and heaved to his feet. "I'll make the call now," he said. "I don't suppose there's any detail you forgot to tell me, is there? Like the license plate of the car, for instance."

"Don't get sore at me," I said. "After all, you're a professional at this, I'm not."

"God knows," he said. He went away to another room to use the phone, and for a while I could hear him muttering and murmuring in there. Karen came back from the kitchen during this, carrying drinks, and the two of us sat in the living room and made small talk about the weather and television and so on while waiting for Reilly to come back.

I found that I liked Karen Smith very much. She was a stunningly beautiful girl, and normally I think stunningly beautiful girls have a way of cramping conversation on first meeting—not that it's *their* fault—but Karen was different. She had such an open manner, such easy humor, that it was easy to relax with her, as though we'd been casual buddies for years.

Reilly spoiled the mood, on his return, by being gruff and impatient, exactly as he'd been when he'd left. "They'll want to talk to you again," he said, coming in, and sat down next to Karen on the sofa.

I said, "Who? Those detectives?"

"Right. Call them in the morning and make arrangements. Early in the morning."

"I will," I promised.

He said, "The other thing is, you better find some place else to stay for a while."

"You mean, not go home?"

"They've got your place staked out," he said. "That's obvious. With any luck you've shaken them now, let's try and keep it that way."

"You think I ought to go to a hotel?"

"Some friend's place would be better," he said. "Somebody they wouldn't think of."

"If it's a friend," I said, "they'd think of it."

Karen said, "You could stay here, if you want. The sofa's comfortable."

"Oh, no," I said. "I wouldn't want to put you out."

"No problem," she assured me. "I have more space here than I need, we wouldn't get in each other's way at all."

"I'll stay in a hotel," I said. "That's all right. Thank you anyway."

Reilly said, "Wait a second, wait a second." He turned to Karen. "You sure it's okay?"

She spread her hands. "Why not? I work all day, half the time I've got dates in the evening, the place is empty practically all the time."

I said, "Really, I appreciate it, but—"

"Shut up," Reilly told me. He leaned closer to Karen, lowered his voice slightly, and said, "You know one thing it means."

She blushed, and smiled, and then we all knew the one thing it meant. She turned toward him and murmured, "There's still your place."

I was beginning to be embarrassed. "Uh," I said. "I'll stay at a hotel. I'd really rather stay at a hotel."

Reilly turned to me and said, "You would. Listen, Fred. Number one, nobody knows you even know Karen, so nobody will look for you here. Number two, you're already here, so you won't have to do any traveling out on the streets. Number three, if you're here Karen and I can both keep an eye on you."

I said, "You want me to stay?"

"I wouldn't say that, exactly," he said. "But I know it's best. So do it."

I looked at Karen. "Are you sure?"

"The place is yours," she said.

"Well. Thank you."

She got to her feet. "Shall I get you another drink?"

"I think you'd better," I said.

TWELVE

The two days I spent in Karen's apartment were among the oddest of my entire life. She did have a large place, as she'd said, but even a large apartment is a relatively small area when two people are living in it, and the first part of my stay was full of abrupt embarrassments, flashes of leg, confusions in the hallway, and excessive politeness on all sides.

The embarrassments began promptly on Saturday night, about half an hour after it had been decided I would stay there. Reilly and Karen began to look cow-eyed at each other, I began to get very much a fifth-wheel feeling, and when finally Reilly suggested to Karen that they "go out" for a while I was as relieved at the idea as they were.

After they left, of course, I felt a little eerie being alone in a strange apartment, and with some sheepishness I went around to every room and turned all the lights on. I spent a fruitless hour or so trying to figure out why anyone would want to kill Uncle Matt and me, and wondering why after two weeks the police couldn't seem to manage to solve the case. As boredom began to get a really good grip on me, I scrounged around the apartment until I found paper and pencil, then sat down in the living room and began to make up a crossword puzzle, something I hadn't done since high school. Back when I was fifteen and sixteen years old I actually sold a number of crossword puzzles to magazines specializing in that sort of thing. I still remember the definition of which at the time I was the proudest: "The poet's on the pumpkin." Five letters.

After a while I gave up the crossword puzzle, watched television instead, and ultimately went to sofa about midnight, falling asleep with less trouble than I'd anticipated.

And Karen, heels in hand and a trifle drunk, inadvertently woke me a little after two when she came in and switched on the living-room light before she remembered she had a house guest. Then, as long as I was awake anyway, and since she had a hankering to talk, we sat awhile and chatted, me in underwear and blanket and she in tight knit dress and stockinged feet.

She wanted to talk about Reilly, mostly, wondering how long I'd known him and what did I think of him and so on. "I can't help it," she told me. "I'm out of my mind for that man, absolutely off my head."

"Are you two going to, uh, get married?"

"Ah, well," she said, and looked tragic, and I knew I'd just made a bad mistake.

I tried to save the situation, saying, "Yes, I remember the first time I ever met Reilly, in the Bunco—" But it was too late; I'd pushed the button and I was going to get the recorded announcement whether I wanted it or not.

"Don't you know about Jack?" she asked me. Because she was tipsy, her speech had great precision in the middle but got fuzzy out around the edges. "Don't you know about his wife?" she asked.

"You mean he's married? Now? Already?"

"Separated. For years and years and years." She gestured, waving away hosts of years. "Separated, but no divorce." She leaned toward me, making her balance in the chair precarious, and whispered confidentially, "Religious problems."

"Oh," I said. "I didn't know that. Reilly never mentioned— but I guess he wouldn't—I mean, he doesn't—uhhh—it wouldn't come up, I suppose. Between him and me."

"Religious problems," she whispered again, and winked at me, and sat back in the chair. "So here I sit," she said. "Completely out of my skull over that man, and nothing to be done. Nothing to be done."

"That's too bad," I said. What else can you say to something like that at two in the morning when you've been awakened in a strange living room by a beautiful woman who's had too much to drink? And who isn't yours?

Well, we talked awhile longer, and then she staggered off to bed, and I disarranged myself on the sofa once again and slept poorly but dreamlessly until seven in the morning, when someone began to dent garbage cans in the areaway.

That was Sunday, the morning our ménage scaled undreamed-of heights of awkwardness. It seemed as though I couldn't turn a corner without running into Karen dressing or undressing or adjusting or bathing or scratching or burping, and it also seemed as though every time she lurched through a doorway I was on the other side just about to put the second leg of my pants on.

In the long run, though, this rotten morning was beneficial. After a couple of hours of it, we were so inured to one another's presence that by mutual unspoken agreement we just stopped getting flustered about it all. No more gulps, no more pardon mes, no more abruptly slammed doors. We relaxed with one another, and promptly the embarrassing situations themselves came to a stop.

After breakfast we made up a shopping list. I was going to be needing things—all sorts of things from socks to a toothbrush—and Karen thought it best if I kept out of sight, so we made up a list and she went shopping for me. The doorbell rang while she was gone, but I didn't answer it. It kept ringing and I kept not answering it. Finally it stopped, and when Karen came back in a minute later Reilly was with her. Reilly said to me, "What's the matter with you now? You deaf?"

"I was playing it safe," I said.

He grumbled.

I asked him if the police were getting anywhere, and how much longer he thought I'd have to stay here, and he told me grumpily he didn't think anyone in the world was getting anywhere with anything, and he supposed I'd be living in Karen's apartment the rest of my life. He then took Karen away with him—for a ride in the country, they said—and I was left to my own devices.

I had the apartment to myself again, and wandered around it with all the boredom I could muster. I read a *Cosmopolitan,* I read a Cheerios box, I read the medicine cabinet. I turned on the television set and switched back and forth for a while without finding anything. I stood at the living-room window and looked out at the gray brick walls and black windows facing me all around, looked down at the concrete areaway at the bottom with its array of dented garbage cans, looked up at the angular triangle of gray sky visible above the roofs, and wound up looking at my own pale reflection in the glass. Even that got dull after a while, so I went to the bedroom and opened the closet doors and poked through all the dresser drawers; not to be nosy, but just for something to do. Karen had what I would consider a lot of clothes. There was also a faint and musky perfume hovering over all her things, and it soon drove me back to the neuter corner of the living room again, where I set to work once more on the crossword puzzle, in which I found myself tending to use words I shouldn't use.

Karen came back at about one-thirty in the morning, arriving just as I was taking the second leg of my pants off. Since Reilly wasn't with her, since I was going to bed no matter what, and since we weren't worrying about that sort of thing any more, I continued to take my pants off, hung them over a chair, and said, "How are you?"

"Dreadful," she said, and began to weep buckets.

Well, what could I do? I went over and put my arms around her and consoled her, and there I stood in my shorts while Karen wept onto my shoulder and told me how she couldn't stand it any more, being *with* Reilly but not *of* Reilly, having to lead this double-life or half-life or whatever it was, and I said, "That's too bad," which seemed to be the only thing I ever said to her after sundown, and in a while she raised her tear-stained face and I kissed her.

It wasn't actually a long kiss, but it would do. When it was over we stood looking at each other, wide-eyed, and I said, "I'm sorry, I shouldn't have done that."

She smiled wanly and said, "You're very sweet, Fred," and turned away and went snuffling off to bed, and I went to sofa, and silence reigned.

Monday morning, nothing was said about last night's kiss. In fact, about all Karen said to me was, "I forgot to tell you, Jack says the two men from Homicide are coming to see you today." She also said she was going to be late for work, but I think she was talking to herself rather than me; in any case, five minutes later she'd torn out of the apartment and I was alone again. Back I went to the sofa, to rest and wait for my vaudeville team from Homicide.

The doorbell rang about quarter to ten, but when I went to the voicebox and asked who was there, I got no answer. I kept saying, "Hello? Hello?" until the doorbell rang a second time, and I realized it was the hall door they were at, not the door downstairs.

Except it wasn't them. I opened the door and an elderly Jewish man was there, dressed in black, with a flat black hat and a long gray beard. He squinted at me and muttered something in what I took to be Yiddish, and I said, "I think you've got the wrong apartment." He consulted a grubby scrap of paper in his palm, turned away from me, and went shuffling toward an apartment across the hall. I shrugged, shut the door, and went back to sofa. But I was awake now, so I turned on the television set and watched a quiz show with celebrities.

The bell rang again ten minutes later. The upstairs bell. I switched off the set, went to the door, and once again it wasn't the police.

Instead, it was a chipper young man with a clipboard. "Hello there, sir," he said brightly, and consulted his clipboard. "I believe a Miss Karen Smith lives here?"

"She isn't in right now," I said.

"Ah. Well, she may have told you I'd be calling."

"She didn't say anything," I said.

He raised an eyebrow. "Mitchell?" he suggested. "Neighborhood Beautification Committee?"

"No, I'm sorry," I said. "She didn't say anything at all."

"That does create a problem," he said, tapping his pencil against his clipboard. "We have her down here for a fifteen-dollar donation. She didn't leave the money with you?"

I felt obscurely as though he half-believed I'd been given the money and was planning to keep it. I said, "No, she didn't leave anything, didn't even mention it."

"Mmm. That's ungood. All this stuff has to be in by noon today."

I remembered having seen some bills tucked away in a

change purse in a bureau drawer in Karen's bedroom. I said, "Just a minute. I may be able to get the money for you."

There was more than enough there, over thirty dollars. I took three fives and gave them to the man at the door. "Thank you, sir," he said. "Here, I'll give you the receipt, you'll need that for tax purposes. Do I make it out to you or Miss Smith?"

"Miss Smith," I said.

He wrote out the receipt and gave it to me and I went back to lie down on the sofa again.

Twenty minutes later I sat up and looked at the receipt on the coffee table beside me. Fifteen dollars! I'd just bought another receipt!

And this time I hadn't even used my own money.

I dashed from the apartment and ran up and down the stairwell, checking all the halls, but of course he was gone.

I'd have to replace that money, but how? I didn't have enough cash on me, and to give her a check I'd have to admit having poked through her personal things. But I couldn't just permanently steal fifteen dollars from her.

I went back to the apartment and paced the living room and thought about it, and I promised myself—as I had done once or twice in the past—that from now on I was going to be *suspicious*.

Sure.

At eleven-thirty the doorbell rang again, the street bell this time, and this time it was actually Steve and Ralph. When they came up they let me know they were unhappy about my not calling them right away when I'd been shot at, but I apologized and said I knew they were right and it wouldn't happen again, so they dropped the subject and went on to other things.

Such as why anybody would want to kill little me. Ralph said, "What we like to do, Fred, you understand, we like to start with a theory, just to have a place to start."

Steve said, "Kind of a direction to move in, Ralph means."

"That's what I mean," agreed Ralph. "Naturally, if in the subsequent investigation we happen to run across facts that don't fit in with this theory, we change the theory."

"Or maybe sometimes the facts," Steve said, and he and Ralph both laughed.

When he was done laughing, Ralph said, "Now, in this particular case we do have a theory. About the guy that shot at you last night."

"Our theory," said Steve, "is he's the same guy that did for your uncle."

"That's just our theory," Ralph explained. "Admittedly, it's got features we aren't too crazy about."

"Like modus operandi, for instance," said Steve.

Ralph looked at Steve and frowned. "Steve," he said, "I don't think Fred is really interested in this sort of technical details. I think what he's more interested in is what you might call the overall design."

"In other words," said Steve, "the theory."

"Exactly," said Ralph. He looked at me, raised his eyebrows, and said, "Well?"

I looked back at him, having no idea what he wanted, and said, "Well what?"

"Well, what do you think of the theory?"

Steve added, "We'd like your opinion of it, Fred, since you're involved, you might say."

I shrugged and said, "I guess it sounds all right. It makes sense, the same person both times."

Ralph said, "Why, Fred?"

"What?"

"You say it makes sense, the same guy killed your Uncle Matt and shot at you. Why does it make sense?"

"Well," I said, at a loss, and instead of finishing the sentence I waved my hands around a little. "It just makes sense, that's all," I said.

"Less sloppy," Ralph suggested. "One murderer for the whole thing. Like a blanket policy."

"I suppose so," I said.

Ralph said, "Then he'd have the same reason, I guess, both times. Kill your uncle, kill you, both the same motive."

"It might be," I said. I had the uncomfortable feeling these two wanted to trap me somehow, but I didn't know where or why.

Steve said, "What do you figure, Fred? Is he after the money?"

"I don't know," I said. "I don't know who he is or what he's after."

"But that looks like a good bet, doesn't it? Maybe he's some second cousin, he figures he'll just keep bumping people off till he inherits."

"That doesn't make any sense," I said. "It'd be too obvious."

Ralph said, "Then let's try another theory. He doesn't want to kill you for your money, Fred, he wants to kill you to shut you up."

Steve smiled happily and said, "How's about that one, Fred? Better?"

"Shut me up? Shut me up from saying what?"

Ralph said, "You tell us, Fred."

Well, I couldn't tell them, which made them unhappy again. We went around in circles awhile longer and finally they left, telling me to keep in touch and to let them know if I moved anywhere else. I promised I would, and sat down on the sofa, and started a new crossword puzzle.

At ten minutes to three that afternoon the phone rang. I

picked it up and a muffled male voice said, "Fred Fitch?"

"Yes?"

"So there you are," he said, and chuckled, and the phone clicked as he hung up.

THIRTEEN

Gertie opened the door and said, "Well, if it isn't the Eagle Scout. How's your knots coming?"

"Loose," I said, and stepped into her apartment. "I don't think I was followed," I said.

She raised a caustic eyebrow. "Not followed! How do you stand such obscurity?"

I said, "Would you like to hear what's been happening, or would you rather go on with this endless chain of exit lines?"

"Well, you're nasty for a ninety-seven-pound weakling," she said, "I'll say that much for you. Come on to the kitchen, I'm making supper."

This apartment, on West 112th Street down the block from St. John's Cathedral, was much smaller and cheaper than Karen's place, and not at all like my own neat den on 19th Street, but I felt immediately at home in it, and shortly found myself sitting with my elbows on the kitchen table, a white mug of coffee in front of me, as I filled Gertie in on what had been happening to me since I'd put her into a cab Saturday night. When I got to the part about the telephone call from the muffled male voice she turned away from the cheese sauce she was making and said, "How'd they get onto you?"

"I don't know. But when I got the call, I panicked. All I could think of was I had to find someplace else to go, and fast. I couldn't go back home, they might still be watching there. I didn't want to take the time to call the police or anything, because I didn't know how close these people already were. They could have been calling from the drugstore on the corner."

"So you called your old pal Gertie," she said.

"I remembered I still had your phone number in my wallet. I called and you said come up and here I am."

"Here you are." She nodded. "Little man," she said, "you've had a busy week. So what now?"

"Now I call Reilly," I said.

"Are you sure?"

I looked at her. "Why not?"

"I still ask you how they got onto you. You never knew this Smith broad till Saturday, so how'd they know you were there?"

I winced at her calling Karen a broad, but I also considered the import of her question. I said, "Reilly? Not Reilly."

"Why not? He hates money?"

"Reilly's my friend," I said.

"Honey," she said, "there's something your Uncle Matt used to say, and he was right. 'A man with half a million bucks can't afford friends.' Money changes things, that's my words of wisdom for today."

"Reilly wouldn't do a thing like that," I said.

"I'm glad to hear it. How'd they get onto you?"

"I don't know. Maybe your friends Steve and Ralph."

She nodded judiciously. "Could be. I never figured those two were exactly priests."

I felt a chill breeze blow across the back of my neck. I said, "What you're saying is, I can't trust anybody in the world."

"You got a pretty way with a phrase, honey," she said.

"So you don't think I should call Reilly or anybody else and tell them I'm here."

"Not unless you want another phone call. Or maybe this time a visit in person. Which believe me, sweetheart, I don't want. Not here. The landlord's down on show-biz people as it is."

"Then what should I do?"

"Stick here till it blows over," she said. "I can get you an army cot from someplace, we'll work it out."

"How will it blow over? When's it going to be safe?"

"When they get the guy knocked off your Uncle Matt. He's the one behind all this, that's the safest bet of the month."

"But what if they never get him?"

"They'll get him. He keeps doing things, agitating, moving around. A guy that can't quit, him they'll get."

"I hope you're right," I said.

"Sure I'm right."

But I wasn't convinced, one way or the other. On the one side I felt I should call Reilly right away—or, instead of Reilly, Steve and Ralph—and tell him what had happened and where I was now, because if the police didn't know what was going on, how could they possibly help me? On the other side there was the problem of how the killer had found out where I was, and the real possibility that Gertie was right, that I could trust absolutely no one now that I was a hundredthousandaire.

I couldn't think about it yet, I was still too confused. So I changed the subject, asking Gertie to tell me about my Uncle Matt, which she was more than willing to do. As he came across in her exuberant description, he was a happy-go-lucky sharpie with a heart full of larceny but without any vestige of a mean streak, a chipper, quick-witted con man with a deck of cards in one hand and a stack of uranium stock in the other, a heavy drinker but not a sloppy one, a big spender and a good-time Charlie, a man whose sense of responsibility and need for security were about as well developed as that of the lilies of the field.

"He made it big down there in Brazil," she said. "Him and Professor Kilroy. He never talked about it much, how he did it, but I knew him before he went south and he never had that kind of cabbage before in his life. I figure he must of hit a couple of those absconding big businessmen, those Wall Street tycoons that duck out to Brazil with a million or two when things get hot. And when he come back he was already sick, he knew he could go any day, and he was what you might call retired. He did some like consultant work for kak, but that was just for kicks."

"For what? He did what?"

"Consultant work," she said.

"No," I said, "the other word. Kak?"

"Oh, yeah. Citizens Against Crime, you heard of them."

"I did?"

"They're one of these reform outfits," she said negligently. "You see about them in the paper all the time."

"I didn't recognize the name," I explained. "What was it you called it? Kak?"

"C," she spelled, "A, C. Kak. Citizens Against Crime."

"Okay," I said. "I've got it now."

"You are fast," she said, not entirely as though she meant it.

I said, "What did Uncle Matt do for, uh, kak?"

"Told em about cons, how the stores work these days and like that."

"Oh. So he wasn't actually working anywhere."

"Naw. Strictly retired, Matt was. Used to play gin some-times, with me or the elevator man, just to keep his hand in, but he had the shakes so bad the last couple of years he couldn't even deal seconds any more."

"Deal seconds?"

"Dealing the second card from the top," she explained. "When Matt was on, sauced just enough and in his health, he could deal fifths all night long and you'd never hear a rustle."

"Fifth card from the top?"

"You know it," she said, and the doorbell rang.

We looked at each other. She said, "Just keep cool and don't make a sound."

"I won't," I promised.

She left the kitchen. I sat at the table and didn't make a sound.

High on one wall was the kind of white plastic kitchen electric clock you get for trading stamps. It had a red sweep second hand, which I watched go round fifteen times, then didn't watch for a while, then watched five times more.

When I figured half an hour had gone by, and when in all that time I hadn't heard a sound from the front of the apart-ment, I went investigating, moving cautiously through the rooms, listening, pausing, looking around corners.

The apartment was empty. The hall door was ajar. I went to it and peeked outside and the hall was also empty, except that lying on the floor out there, on its side, was a shoe made entirely of white plastic straps and a red plastic wedgie heel.

The other one must still have been on Gertie's foot.

FOURTEEN

Now what?

I stood in the middle of Gertie's crowded messy tiny living room, I held Gertie's wedgie in my right hand, and I asked myself that question aloud: "Now what?"

There was no answer.

When a person has been kidnapped—and with this shoe for mute testimony what else was there to believe but that Gertie had been kidnapped by party or parties (probably parties) unknown?—one's first reaction is, "Call the police!" so that on coming back into the apartment I'd headed straight for the phone. But in the nick of time I'd brought myself up short, remembering something Gertie herself had pointed out to me just a few minutes before she'd disappeared:

Only four people had known I was at Karen Smith's apartment, and three of them were cops.

Dare I call the police? Dare I let the likes of Steve and Ralph know where I was? I'd instinctively mistrusted those two from the very first time I'd met them, and now it seemed probable my instinct had been—for once—correct.

Then what about Reilly? He was my friend, he'd been my friend for years, surely *he* wouldn't betray me.

But hadn't Reilly been acting oddly the last few days, grumpy and sullen and strangely distant? And didn't he turn out to be living some sort of double life, with Karen on one side and an invisible wife on the other? And hadn't I always suspected him of containing at least as much con man as the criminals he was charged with apprehending? Was this a man I could completely trust?

Or what of Karen herself? Hadn't she, on our very first meeting in Madison Square Park, lied to me and gulled me? What did I know about her, after all, other than that she was a convincing liar and was having an affair with a married man?

No, no, I could trust none of these people, not if I valued my skin.

To whom, then, could I turn? I went farther afield, to my so-called lawyer, the brave Attorney Goodkind; *there* was a man I wouldn't trust with a subway token in the Sahara. And when my neighbor Wilkins had come to me with his trunk full of novel had he in actuality been casing the joint for the mob? Was that less unlikely than his claim to have written a book about airborne Roman legions dropping rocks on the primitives of Gaul? And what about Mr. Grant, wasn't he in a way too good to be true, melting into the background, seeming so meek and inoffensive, the surest sign of the archconspirator? Couldn't he or Wilkins—or both, why not?—have been planted in my building years ago, just waiting for the right moment?

Was all this far-fetched? Of course it was, but three hundred thousand dollars was far-fetched in the first place. Being shot at and hounded was far-fetched. Gertie's being kidnapped from under my nose was far-fetched. My Uncle Matt's murder was far-fetched.

As far as that went, my Uncle Matt's very *existence* was far-fetched.

And who knew to what lengths some people might not go to get their hands on three hundred thousand dollars?

Very well, Uncle Matt had been right; a man with three hundred thousand dollars can't afford friends. From now on, whatever happened, I would be able to rely on no one but myself.

The thought was not encouraging. I was aware of my capabilities and of my limitations, and I knew which was the longer list.

But what was I to do? And if I didn't even dare *report* Gertie's kidnapping, how would anyone ever find her?

Somehow or other that was now up to me too, and I knew it, and I quailed before the responsibility. How would I go about finding Gertie, and rescuing her, and bringing her kidnappers to justice? How would I even begin? All I knew anything about was library research, and I strongly doubted I'd be finding Gertie in any library.

In true researcher style, I tried marshaling my facts, and found them in short supply. Fogs and suspicions and confusions littered the landscape all around me, but of facts there were very few. Only three, in fact: (1) Gertie had been kidnapped. (2) I had been shot at. (3) Uncle Matt had been murdered.

Was that a starting point, number three? The murder of Uncle Matt actually had been the beginning of all this, so was that where I should begin? At the very least it was, in this sea of shifting ambiguities, a fact that stood firm, something that could be studied, something I could be sure of: my Uncle Matt *had* been murdered.

Had he?

Oh, come *on.* After all, *something* had to be true. If you couldn't believe anything at all, how could you move, how could you think, how could you act? It was necessary to start somewhere.

I had meandered this far in my thinking when the doorbell suddenly shrilled and I leaped at once to attention. Could this be them? Could they have found out—perhaps by torturing Gertie—that I was here, and had they returned to get me?

My initial impulse was to hide in the nearest closet or under the nearest bed, shut my eyes, and wait for them to go away. In fact, I even took a quick tiptoeing step toward the rear of the apartment before I remembered that I *wanted* to see them, that I'd just been straining my brain to think of a way to *find* them. If now they had come to me, so much the better.

At least that's what I told myself, while glancing in quick panic around the room for some sort of weapon; after all, I was out to capture them, not to let them capture me.

Atop the television set in one corner of the living room was a lamp of such monumental ugliness as to be magnificently impressive, like Chicago. Its porcelain base represented an endless chain of Cupids, in white and pink and gold, doing things together. It may all have been very obscene, there was no real way to be sure. At any rate, I hurried over and removed this monstrosity's fringed shade, pulled its cord from the wall plug, and hefted the lamp in my right hand, finding it pleasingly weighty. Holding this weapon of love behind my back I went over and opened the door, ready to start smashing Cupids into every face I saw.

The gray-haired, full-jowled, black-suited minister on the threshold smiled sweetly upon me and said, in a soft and gentle voice, "Good afternoon to you, my dear sir. Would Miss Gertrude Divine be at home?"

Was the lamp really out of sight? Flustered, jamming the lamp into the small of my back, I said, "Well, no, she isn't.

She had to, uh, go out for a while. I don't know exactly when she'll be back."

"Ah, well," he said, and sighed, and transferred the brown paper package from his right arm to his left. "I'll try again another time," he said. "My apologies for having intruded."

Anything might have relevance, anything at all, so I said, "Could you tell me what it was about?"

"Mr. Grierson's Bible," he said. "Perhaps I could come back tomorrow afternoon."

"I'm not sure she'll be here," I said. "What do you mean, Mr. Grierson's Bible?"

"The Bible he ordered, the inscribed Bible."

So Uncle Matt, the famous boulevardier and con man, had gotten religion toward the end. It was small of me, I know, but I found myself taking a nasty little pleasure in the thought of the supremely confident confidence man losing some of that confidence as he saw the end approaching.

I think I managed to hide this unworthy pleasure as I said, "I'm Mr. Grierson's nephew, maybe I could help."

"Ah, are you?" His smile of pleasure was tinged with sadness as he said, "I am most happy to meet you, sir, though one could wish it were under happier circumstances. I am the Reverend Willis Marquand."

"How do you do? I'm Fredric Fitch. Won't you, uh, won't you come in?"

"If you're sure I'm not disturbing you?"

"Not at all, sir."

Reverend Marquand noticed the lamp as I was closing the door. I held it up and laughed foolishly and said, "Just putting this up when you rang." I went over and put it back in its place on the television set, then offered Reverend Marquand a seat.

When we were both seated, he said, "A real loss, your uncle. A fine man."

"You knew him well?"

"Only telephonically, I'm afraid. We chatted awhile when he phoned the Institute to order the Bible." He patted the brown paper package, now resting on the sofa beside him.

"Is that it?"

"Would you care to see it? It's our finest model, and really beautiful. We're all quite proud of it."

He removed the wrappings and showed it to me, and it was impressive in much the same way as the lamp, and with the same color scheme. It was bound in white leatherette with an ornate gilt cross on the front and ornate gilt lettering on the spine. The page edges were all gilt, and gold and red ribbons were available to mark one's place. Inside, intricately illuminated letters were the rule, ornate brightly colored illustrations on heavy glossy paper were scattered throughout, and much of the dialogue was in red. The first page was inscribed in flowing gilt script:

> To Dearest Gertrude,
> with all my love forever
> Whither Thou Goest, I Will Go
> Ruth 1:16
>
> Matthew Grierson

Now, this was odd. I could visualize Uncle Matt turning to religion himself in his old age, particularly knowing he was suffering from terminal cancer, but that he or anybody else would consider a gold and white leatherette Bible the right gift for Gertie Divine—despite her name—was hard to believe. There was more here than met the eye.

Then I understood. This was a message of some kind, a clue that Gertie would understand.

A clue to what?

Well, maybe three hundred thousand dollars wasn't all there was to it. After all, Brazil was where Uncle Matt made his money, and Brazil is a great new raw nation, its wealth hardly tapped. Maybe there was more, much more, and the three hundred thousand was only the visible part of the iceberg, and the clue to the rest of it was somehow here in this Bible.

Of course! Why else give the three hundred thousand to a perfect stranger, even if he is technically a relative? Because it's chicken feed, because the really *big* money is tied up somewhere else.

That's why Uncle Matt sent Gertie to me. He was leaving it up to her whether she would tell me about the rest of it or not. The three hundred thousand was a kind of test, to see if I was worthy of all of it. And Gertie had been kidnapped by people intent on forcing the information out of her.

I said, "You're delivering this, is that it?"

"Well—" He smiled in some embarrassment. "There is the question of payment. Your uncle was to have sent us a check, but unfortunately he passed on before—"

"Well, how much is it?"

"Thirty-seven dollars and fifty cents."

"I'll write you a check," I said. I'd brought along my checkbook when I'd first left home, not knowing how long I'd be gone, but this was the first time I'd had to use it so far.

Reverend Marquand loaned me a pen and said, "Just make it out to Dear Hearts Institute."

I wrote out the check and gave it to him, and he seemed ready to settle down, ministerlike, and discuss my own religious affiliations with me at some length. I begged off, saying I did have some work to get done, and he was very good about it, leaving at once and letting me get to the job of studying the Bible.

I spent nearly an hour at it, and got nowhere. How was this Bible different from all other Bibles? I couldn't figure it out. But of course Gertie was the one the message was for, and I had no doubt it would be meaningful to her in one glance.

Finally I had to give it up. I hid the Bible in the oven, put it completely out of my mind, and went back to the train of thought I'd been on when the Reverend Marquand had arrived, which had been the decision that the only fact of which I could be at all sure was the murder of Uncle Matt. Starting from there, and with the luck of a Daily Double winner, maybe I could eventually find some other facts about which to be sure.

Very well. I left a note for Gertie, telling her I'd phone in from time to time just in case she should escape from her captors, and went out to look up the murder reports in the newspapers at the library.

The Lone Researcher was on the trail.

FIFTEEN

The *Daily News* found my Uncle Matt dull, but didn't like to say so. He was, after all, a semimysterious old demimillionaire with an oddball will and a weird history and a photogenic ex-stripper nurse, and as if that weren't enough, he'd also been murdered in his luxury penthouse apartment on Central Park South and the murderer was still at large. It was clear the *News* felt it *should* have a field day with Uncle Matt, and yet somehow it just couldn't seem to get a good grip on him. Every item that started out to be a story about Uncle Matt's murder ultimately wound up being a story about something else instead, usually the Collier brothers, with whom my uncle, so far as I could tell, had shared no characteristics at all, other than being dead, having money and belonging to the white race.

Still, the *Daily News* was the only game in town. The *Times* had given the story one bare useless item the day after the murder, and the other papers had been almost as bad. Only the *News* had persisted in follow-up stories, I suppose out of a sense of noblesse oblige.

Ah, well. Intermixed with the references to Jack London and Peaches Browning (don't ask *me* how they did it) I did find the facts of the case, such as they were, and copied them laboriously into the notebook I'd just bought for the purpose.

Uncle Matt had been murdered the night of Monday, May 8, seventeen days ago. Gertie had gone out to a movie that evening with a friend identified as one Gus Ricovic and hadn't returned to the apartment until one-thirty in the morning, at which time she discovered the body and phoned the police. The actual murder was assumed to have taken place somewhere between ten and eleven. Death had resulted from a single blow to the back of the head made by some blunt instrument, not found on the premises nor turned up in the subsequent investigation. There was no sign of forcible entry into the apartment, nor was there any indication of a fight or any other struggle. So far as Gertie knew (or at least so far as she had told the police and reporters), Uncle Matt hadn't expected any visitors that evening.

The *Daily News* was so taken with the notion of someone murdering a man who's expected to die momentarily from cancer anyway that they even interviewed Uncle Matt's doctor, one Lucius Osbertson, who from his manner in the interview I took to be both rotund and orotund; in the spaces between the lines Dr. Osbertson could faintly be heard lamenting the loss of a steady source of fees.

The follow-up stories added little. The police appeared to be wandering dispiritedly in an ever-diminishing spiral, like a band of defeatist Indians who've lost their warpath. Gertie came in for a lot of attention, with photos and interviews and her show-biz biography. Gus Ricovic was never mentioned at all after the initial story. Here and there references were made to the strange will Uncle Matt was supposed to have left behind, but of course its details had not as yet been made public, so there were no references to me, and by the time I would have been available for the spotlight the story was as dead as Uncle Matt. By the sixth day after the murder, in fact, even the *Daily News* had nothing left to say about it anymore.

When I left the newspaper library, my new notebook bristling with the facts in the case, it was five o'clock, the height of that daily self-torture known as the rush hour. I was on 43rd Street west of Tenth Avenue and decided it would be saner to walk than to try to find a cab or squeeze myself aboard a Ninth Avenue bus, so walk is what I did. It was probably also quicker; I made it, walking at a leisurely pace, in twenty-five minutes, and so far as I could tell I wasn't shot at once.

I had thought at first, while in the library, of going back to Gertie's place, of maybe using that as my base of operations, but then it seemed to me that Gertie might be forced into admitting that I'd been there, and in that case her kidnappers would naturally stake the place out on the assumption that I'd be back. After that I'd considered staying at a hotel, but the idea of signing a false name to a hotel register while a desk clerk stood directly in front of me and looked at me was far too nerve-racking to consider. As to staying with some friend, my friends were too few and precious for me to want to involve any of them in kidnappings and murder attempts, not to mention the fact that God alone knew if I could trust any of them.

When all was said and done, there was only one place I could go and that place was home. My own apartment. Surely no one would expect to find me in my own apartment, so it was unlikely that anyone would be looking for me there, and that meant I could expect to be at least as safe there as anywhere else in the world. And a good deal more comfortable; I could change my suit, I could sleep in my own bed, I could begin to lead again at least some small remnant of my former life.

Thus went my thinking, and I could find no flaws in it. Still and all, as I approached my own block my feet did begin to drag a little, my shoulders to hunch, and the small of my back just slightly to itch. I found myself peering into every parked car, and flinching away from every moving one. I alternately stared into the faces of pedestrians coming the other way or ducked my own face behind my hand, neither tactic being particularly brilliant since I left in my wake a long line of immobile pedestrians standing flat-footed on the sidewalk and staring after me. As a result, my return was not entirely as unobtrusive as I had hoped it might be.

Nevertheless, I came to my own building without incident, and entered, and found my mailbox filled to overflowing. Actually overflowing; letters were sticking out of the slot above the door like darts out of a dartboard. When I unlocked the little door it sprang open with a sound like *phong!*, only faster, and a whole wad of mail burst out and scattered all over the floor.

I filled my jacket pockets with letters, held another stack in my left hand, and went on upstairs. As I reached the second-floor landing, the door there opened, Wilkins appeared, and the two of us faced each other for the first time since Gertie had thrown him—and his suitcase—out of my apartment. Wilkins raised his ink-stained hand, pointed a rigid ink-stained finger at me, and said, icily, "Just you wait." Then he snapped the door shut again.

I hesitated there on the landing, wanting to knock on that slammed door and see if I could make it up to Wilkins somehow, because after all I did truly owe him an apology. The very worst that could be said of the man was that he was deluded, and if I had come perilously close to entering his delusion that was my fault, not his. And I did have more money now than I could possibly use, so why not put some of it into the publication of his novel, regardless of whether or not it was any good?

But there was no time for all that now, so making a mental note to talk to Wilkins when the rest of this was all over, I went on past his door and up the stairs to the third floor and walked into my apartment.

Where a woman with impossibly red hair, sequined tortoise-shell glasses and a mostly-yellow plaid suit leaped up from my reading chair, flung her arms out, and came rushing toward me on spike-heel shoes, beaming and crying, "Darling! I'm here and the answer is yes!"

SIXTEEN

I didn't even know what the question was. Quickly I side-stepped the embrace, ran around the sofa, and with a little distance between us said, "What now? What's all this?"

She had turned, like the bull still after the cape, and paused on tippy-heel, arms still outflung as she cried, "Darling, don't you *recognize* me? Have I changed so much?"

Was there really something familiar about her, or was it merely the old suggestibility at work again? Taking no chances, I said, "Madam, I have never seen you before in my life. Explain yourself. What are you doing here?"

"Darling, I'm *Sharlene!*"

"Sharlene?" I squinted, trying to get the picture. There had been a Sharlene back in high school, a shy little girl I'd managed to go steady with for a while, a wistful ephemeral little thing who'd had it in her head she wanted to be a poetess. Most of the kids in school had called her Emily Dickinson, which she had taken as a compliment.

"Sharlene *Kester!*" yelled this garden-club monstrosity, giving in truth the full name of that frail girl-child.

"You?" In my bafflement I actually pointed at her. "*You're* Emily Dickinson?"

"You *remembered!*" The thought so enraptured her that she charged me again, arms outstretched as though she were doing her impression of a Flying Fortress, and it was only the nimblest of footwork that enabled me to keep the sofa between us.

I shouted, "Wait a minute, *wait* a minute!" I held up my hand like a traffic cop.

Amazingly enough, she stopped. Tilted somewhat forward, seemingly ready to leap into action again at any instant, she inquired, "Darling, what is it? I'm here, I'm yours, the answer is yes! Why don't you take me?"

"Answer?" I asked. "Answer to what?"

"Your letter!" she cried. "That beautiful beautiful letter!"

"What letter? I didn't write you any letter."

"The letter from *camp.* I know how long it's been, believe me I know, but you told me to take my time, to answer only when I was sure, and now I'm sure. The answer is *yes!*"

My mind was empty. I said, in bafflement, "Camp?"

"Boy Scout camp!" Then, abruptly, the manic look on her face switched to something much sterner, and in a quick cold voice she said, "You aren't going to say you didn't *write* that letter."

Then I remembered. The summer I was fifteen I had spent two weeks in a Boy Scout camp, two of the most disastrous weeks of my life; of all the gear I'd taken to camp with me, I'd returned with nothing but my left sneaker, and it without its laces. That was also the year I'd been going steady with Sharlene Kester, and in a fit of depression while at camp I had written her a letter; yes, I had. But what the letter had said I could no longer remember at all.

Nor could I understand why, sixteen years later, Sharlene—

could this gaily daubed hippo really be Sharlene?—why she should out of a clear blue sky decide to answer that letter.

Unless she'd heard about the inheritance. Eh? Eh?

While I was wasting time thinking, Sharlene was still talking. She was saying, "Just let me tell you something, Fred Fitch. You remember my Uncle Mortimer, who used to be assistant district attorney back home? Well, he's a judge now, and I showed him your letter, and he says it's a clear proposal of marriage, and it'll stand up in any court in the United States. And he told me, if you've gone big-city and think you're going to trifle with me, he told me he'll handle the whole thing *himself*, and *you'll* be slapped with a breach of promise suit just faster than you can think, so you'd better be careful what you say to me. Now. Do you remember that letter or don't you?"

No, not this. I didn't have time for this, that's all. I didn't know whether or not Sharlene—my God!—had a case against me, and at the moment I really didn't care. All I knew was that I already had too much to think about and it was time to set the excess wolves at each other's throats for a change. So, "Excuse me," I said, and went over to the telephone.

"You go ahead and call anyone you want to," she said loudly. "I know my rights. You can't trifle with *my* affections."

It was five-thirty by now, and no longer normal office hours, but Goodkind had struck me as the sort of man who'd be liable to stay late in the office, gloating over the law volumes dealing with mortgage foreclosures. If he weren't there, I'd just have to take a chance on calling Reilly.

Fortunately, Goodkind was true to his character and present in his office. When he answered I identified myself, and he said, "Fred! I've been looking all over for you! Where are you?"

"Never mind," I said. "I want to—"

"Are you home?"

"No. I want to—"

"Fred, I've got to talk to you."

"In a minute. I want to—"

"This is important! Vital!"

"I want to—"

"Can you come to the office?"

"No. I want to—"

"We've got to meet, and talk. There are things—"

"God damn it," I shouted, "shut up for a minute!"

There was stunned silence all over the world. Out of the corner of my eye I saw Sharlene staring at me in blank astonishment.

Into the silence, I said, "If you're my attorney, you'll listen to me for one minute. If you don't want to listen, you're not my attorney."

"Fred," said a voice composed entirely of cholesterol, "of course I'll listen to you. Anything, Fred."

"Good. When I was fifteen years old I spent two weeks at a Boy Scout camp."

"Wonderful places," he said, a trifle vaguely, but obviously wanting to please.

"While there," I said, "I wrote a letter to a girl I knew in high school. She's here now, in New York. Her uncle's a judge in Montana. She claims the letter's a proposal of marriage, and if I don't marry her she'll sue me for breach of promise."

I held the phone away from my ear so Sharlene could join me in listening to Goodkind laugh. His laughter reminded me of the witch in Walt Disney's *Snow White.*

Behind her sequined harlequin tortoise-shell spectacles, Sharlene had begun to blink a lot. Her expression had now become nervous, but determined.

When Goodkind was down to little giggles and chuckles, I put the phone back to my head and said, "What should I do?

Should I tell her no?" Then I held the phone out again, so we could both hear his answer.

I must admit the answer surprised me, because what he said was, "Oh, no, not a bit. Fred? Act worried, boy. Bluster if you can. Act as though you don't want to marry her, and you're trying to bluff, and you're afraid you don't have a leg to stand on. If we can con these people into actually taking us to court—" Instead of ending the sentence, he began to giggle again.

I brought the mouthpiece close, and said to my mouth-piece, "What good does that do me?"

"Does her family have any money?" he asked me. "Do they own their house, have a business of any kind?"

"Excuse me a second," I said. "She just left the door open, and there's a draft coming in."

I walked over to the door, and clearly I could hear the tickety-tick of her heels as she raced down the stairs. Then, up the stairwell came the faintly receding cry, "You'll pay for thiiiiisss!!!"

With a feeling rare to me in life—the feeling called triumph—I quietly closed the door.

SEVENTEEN

When I got back to the phone, Goodkind was saying, "Hello? Hello? Hello?"

"Hello," I said.

"*There* you are. Where are you?"

"I'm not at liberty to say right now," I said.

"Fred, it is imperative that we get together—"

He was wrong. What was imperative was that I assume control somehow. Steeling myself, I said, "For the last time, don't call me Fred."

"You can call me Marcus," he said.

"I don't want to call you Marcus," I told him, which may have been the harshest thing I'd ever said to anybody in my life. "I want to call you Mr. Goodkind. I want you to call me Mr. Fitch."

"But . . . but that isn't the way it's done. Everybody calls everybody by his first name."

"Everybody but you and me," I said.

"Well," he said doubtfully, "you're in charge." Which made me glow all over.

Keeping the smile out of my voice, I said, "The other reason I called, I want some money."

"Well, naturally, Fr—uh. Naturally. It's yours."

"Is there any of it you can get hold of without any documents from me?"

"Well, uh—"

"I'm not accusing you of anything," I said. "I just want to know if there's any way you can transfer some funds without my having to sign anything or show up anywhere."

"It would be best if you came here, you know. Or if you want I could meet you some—"

"Is—there—any—way?"

Silence, then: "Yes."

"Good. I want you to take four thousand dollars and put it into my account at Chase Hanover, the branch at Twenty-fifth and Seventh. Just a second, I'll get you my account number."

I went away and looked for my checkbook, found it at last in my jacket pocket, where it had been for the last five days—I didn't seem to be able to think about more than one thing at a time—went back to the telephone, and heard Goodkind saying, with some urgency, "Hello? Hello? Hello?"

"Stop saying hello," I said.

"I thought you'd hung up. Ff—uh. Are you feeling all right?"

"I'm fine. My account number is seven six oh, dash, five nine two, space, six two two nine three, space, eight. Have you got that?"

He read it back to me.

"Good," I said. "Transfer the money first thing tomorrow morning. And do it in cash so I can start drawing on it right away."

"I will," he promised. "Is there anything else?"

"Yes. My uncle's apartment. Has it been rented to anybody else or can I still get into it?"

"It's yours," he said. "Part of the estate. It's a co-op, your uncle owned it."

"Get a set of keys to the doorman," I said. "Tonight," I added, though I had no intention of going there before tomorrow sometime. I was beginning to learn a little bit about subterfuge.

"Will do," he said.

"And when I get there," I told him, "don't you be snooping around."

"I'm your attorney, Ffuff."

"Who?"

"I'm your attorney. There are important things—"

"The keys to the doorman," I said. "That's the important thing."

"I'll do it," he promised. "And now we've got to talk."

"Later," I said, and hung up. I well knew the dangers in allowing me to be talked to.

Evening was coming on by now, and it seemed a good idea to show no light at my windows, just in case, so for the next twenty minutes I went about the task of erecting makeshift blackout curtains, composed of blankets and towels and my bedspread and shower curtain. When I was done, the apartment had a strangely underground appearance, possibly a fall-out shelter for the Budapest String Quartet, but I was reasonably certain no light would show to any watcher outside, and that was the important part.

While I'd been at work the phone had rung several times, once continuing for eighteen rings before the caller had given up. This was my first experience at not answering a telephone and I found it surprisingly difficult, much like giving up smoking. My mind kept trying to betray me, kept insisting that it was unnatural not to answer the telephone (or not to smoke), and I found it physically difficult to stay in the other room. As the evening wore on, the phone sounded a few more times, and it never did get any easier to ignore.

At any rate, once I'd completed the blackout arrangements I took a look at my incredible stack of mail, now piled up on the drop-leaf table near the door. I began by sorting the one stack into three stacks, separated into bills, personal letters and others, and for the first time in my life the smallest stack was of bills. These I immediately tucked away in the bill pigeon-hole in my desk, and then I sat down to see what my personal mail was all about.

It was all about money, though hardly any of my corre-spondents actually used the word. There were seven letters from relatives—four cousins, two aunts and a niece-in-law—none of whom had ever written me a letter before in their lives. The letters were chatty and newsy, in a gimme sort of way: Cousin James Fisher had a golden opportunity to buy a Shell station out to the new highway, and Aunt Arabella needed an operation on her back in the worst way, and Cousin Wilhel-mina Spofford surely wished she could afford to go to the University of Chicago. And so on.

I read all the letters, and I began to backslide. I *wanted* to believe, against all the evidence of the world, that these people were writing to me because they liked me and wanted to be in communication with me, and because I wanted to believe it I came perilously close to letting myself believe it.

In order to fortify myself against my structural weaknesses, when I finished the last of my relations' advertisements for themselves I looked up and spoke aloud. "Bah," I said. "Hum-bug." I then used the seven letters to start a warming little blaze in my fireplace, and sat in front of it to read the third stack of mail, the miscellaneous pile.

The word *miscellaneous* has perhaps never been so aptly employed. This stack included an advertisement for a company that was bound and determined to save me money on slacks if I would only send them my measurements and choice of color, and a notice from a bunch of monks in California alerting me to the news that they intended to say Mass for me en masse every day for the next hundred years and if I wished to express my appreciation for this religious frenzy I could use the enclosed envelope no stamp needed, and a newsletter informing me that the Kelp-Chartle Non-Sectarian Orphanage of Augusta, Georgia, is on the brink of bankruptcy won't I help, and a badly typed note from a man in Baltimore who if I write song lyrics he writes music why don't we get together, and a notice from an organization called Citizens Against Crime (Senator Earl Dunbar, Honorary Chairman)—and wasn't that the outfit Uncle Matt was "consultant" for?—telling me that if I wanted to help stamp out racketeers and gangsters all I had to do was send a check to further CAC's good work, and a form letter from an insurance man who if I would tell him how old I was he would tell me how much money he could save me on life insurance use the enclosed envelope no stamp needed, and half a dozen mixed charity appeals, and a notice that I'd won a free dance lesson, and a notice that I'd won a free crate of Florida oranges, and a letter from a lawyer informing me that his client Miss Linda Lou McBeggle intends to mount a paternity suit against me unless I do right by her having already done wrong by her, and a scented envelope containing a notice about Miss Crystal St. Cyr's at-home massage service, and a warning that I was in big trouble if I didn't give all my money to the Saints Triumphant World Universal Church because it's harder for a rich man to get into Heaven than for a camel to pass through a needle's eye, and a notice that I had a library book overdue.

You know, if I had been approached by any one of these

things separately I would more than likely have fallen for it—if I didn't have so much else on my mind—but having them all piled up together like this was eye-opening, because for the first time I could see just how ridiculous they were. Just as one nude woman is beautiful but a nudist colony is only silly.

How the fire roared.

EIGHTEEN

I set my alarm for nine o'clock, but the telephone woke me at twenty past eight. I was almost groggy enough to answer it, but woke up slowly as I staggered into the living room, and came to consciousness just as my fingers touched the receiver. I jerked my hand back as though the plastic were hot, and stood weaving there until one of the silences between rings stretched and stretched and stretched and changed key and became the silence of an apartment in which no telephone is ringing.

At that point I had my first coherent thought of Tuesday, the twenty-fifth of May: "Now that I have three hundred thousand dollars, I can get an extension phone."

This thought pleased me and I smiled, and then, not to waste the expression, I went into the bathroom and brushed my teeth.

It was hard to believe it was really eight-thirty in the morning, headed for nine o'clock. My blackout curtains were still covering all the windows at both front and rear of the apartment, so that inside it was not very long after midnight. All the while I was preparing breakfast I had to fight the feeling I was actually having a midnight snack, and when at five minutes to ten I went downstairs and out to a bright and sun-shiny world, all this glaring light seemed wrong somehow, the way it does when you've gone to the movies in the middle of the afternoon and you come outside and it's still day. It shouldn't be still day, but it is.

Combined with this feeling of temporal displacement was another, much worse: an itching between the shoulder blades. Though I didn't see that long black limousine awaiting me out front, and though both sidewalks seemed conspicuously empty of conspicuously lounging men, I felt very strange and uneasy about going out into all that bright sunlight, exposing myself as the biggest target in the world. Going down the stoop my mind was full of notions of high-powered rifles on roofs across the way, submachine guns jutting out the windows of parked cars, passing pedestrians suddenly whirling about with blazing automatics in their hands. When I got all the way down to the sidewalk with none of this happening, I actually felt a sense of anticlimax. A welcome anticlimax, but an anticlimax just the same.

I hurried directly to the bank, where I learned that Good-kind had made the exchange of funds for me as I'd asked, and where I cashed a check for a hundred dollars. I also did some heavy peering around, on the possibility that Goodkind might stake out the bank in hopes I'd show up, but he was nowhere in sight. Any number of suspicious characters avoided my eye while I was doing this scanning, but that's normal for New York and didn't mean that any of them were following me or had any connection with me.

I went from the bank to a street-corner phone booth. I had calls to make and I didn't know but what someone might be tapping my line at home to see if I was there. I was pleased at having thought of this precaution and felt almost cheery as I dialed the operator and asked her to connect me with Police Headquarters.

I was far less cheery three and a half minutes later when I finally got someone who would listen to me. An emergency would have to happen very slowly in New York City for a telephone call to the police to have any effect on it. The operator had given me a good long stretch of dead air punctuated by tiny faraway clicks before at last a crashingly loud close-up click shattered my eardrum and heralded the start of ringing. Four rings went by, well spaced, as I sweated in the phone booth, and at last I was in contact with a man with a gravel voice and a Brooklyn accent, who would listen to nothing from me other than my location. I pleaded, I shouted, I started a dozen different sentences, and when at last I gave up and told him the intersection I was calling from, he promptly went away, I was treated to another spate of dead air, and I leaned against the phone-booth glass and watched the cabs go by until a sudden voice said, "Fraggis-Steep Frecinct."

"Oh," I said. "I want to report—"

"Fummation or complaint?" he asked me.

"I beg your pardon?"

He sighed. "You want fummation?" he asked me. "Or you wanna regista complaint?"

"Oh," I said, at last understanding. "Information, you mean!"

"Fummation? Right." Click.

"No!" I cried. "Not fummation! Complaint! Complaint!" But it was too late.

Dead air again, followed by another male voice, this one saying, "Sergeant Srees, Fummation."

"I don't want fummation," I said. "I want to register a complaint."

"You got the wrong office," he told me. "Hold on." And he began clicking very loudly in my ear.

I held the phone away from my head, listened to the tiny clicking, and finally the tiny voices as a male operator came on and was told by my friend of Fummation to switch me over to Complaint. I brought the phone cautiously back to my ear, and after a little more silence, got yet another voice, this one saying, "Sergeant Srees, Desk."

"I want to register a complaint," I said.

"Felony or misdemeanor?"

"What?"

"You wanna regista felony? Or you wanna regista misdemeanor?"

"Kidnapping," I said. "That's a felony, I think."

"You want Tectivision," he told me. "Hang on." And clicked to let me know there was no use talking to him any more.

I did anyway. "You people are crazy," I said into the dead air. "Somebody could steal the whole city, sell it to Chicago, you wouldn't even hear about it till a week later."

"Srees, Tectivision."

"What's that?"

"Tectivision."

I concentrated. "Once more," I said.

"Smatter with you?" he asked me. "You want a Spanish-speakin tective?"

"Detective Division," I said, as the light dawned.

"Hold on," he said, and clicked.

"Wait!" I shouted. A young couple walking past my phone booth flinched. I saw them hurry away, trying not to act as though they were walking very fast. They didn't look back.

"Mendez, Tectivision."

"Look," I said, but before I could say any more he said two

million words in Spanish, all in the space of ten seconds. When he was done I was a little groggy, but I kept trying. "I don't speak Spanish," I said. "Do you have anybody there that speaks English?"

"I speak English," he said, enunciating with beautiful clarity.

"God bless you," I said. "I want to report a kidnapping."

"When did this occur?"

"Yesterday. Her name is Gertrude Divine, she was kidnapped from her apartment yesterday afternoon."

"Your name, sir?"

"This is one of those anonymous calls," I said.

"We must have your name, sir."

"No, no. That's the whole point of an anonymous call, I don't give you my name. Now, Miss Divine's address is 727 West 112th Street, apart—"

"Not this precinct?"

"I beg your pardon?"

"Why are you calling this precinct, sir? This event occurred way uptown. Just a moment, I'll connect you with the correct precinct."

"No, you won't," I said. "I've reported the kidnapping, and now I'm hanging up."

"Sir—"

I hung up.

After this experience I needed to rest my nerves awhile before making my other call, so I left the phone booth and walked a block to another outdoor booth, where I called Dr. Lucius Osbertson, he being Uncle Matt's doctor, the one who'd been interviewed by the *Daily News*. I didn't want to give Dr. Osbertson advance warning that I was coming to see him, just to be on the safe side, so when his receptionist or nurse or whoever she was answered the phone I asked her if the doctor had office hours at all today.

"Twelve till two," she said. "Name, please?"

I panicked, not having a name quick to hand. Staring out the phone-booth glass in desperation, seeing the stores and diners all around me, I opened my mouth and said, "Fred Nedick."

Fred Nedick? What kind of a name was that? I stood there in the phone booth and waited for her to say something like oh-come-off-it, or ha-ha-very-funny, or oh-another-drunk-eh?

Instead, she said, "Has the doctor seen you before, Mr. Nedick?"

This part I *had* prepared in advance. "No," I said. "I was recommended by Dr. Wheelwright." I actually did know a Dr. Wheelwright, who gave me a penicillin shot every February when I got the current year's virus. My feeling was that no doctor would just blindly turn away a patient who claimed a recommendation from another doctor, even if Doctor A didn't recognize the name of Doctor B. (Is any of this making sense?)

The nurse, at any rate, said, "Excuse me one minute, please, Mr. Nedick," and left me standing there under the foolish weight of the name I'd given myself. I scratched myself and felt inadequate and uncomfortable until she returned and said, "The doctor can see you at the end of office hours today. If you could be here at one forty-five?"

"One forty-five. Yes, thank you."

"That's quarter till two."

"Yes," I said, "I know it is."

"Some people get confused," she said. And hung up.

Nineteen

Minetta Lane is an L-shaped street, one block long, in the heart of Greenwich Village. It is a beautiful street, in a Little Old New York sort of way, and is almost the only area that still looks like Greenwich Village, the rest of it looking mostly like Coney Island. Except West 8th Street, which looks like Far Rockaway.

In any case, I was going to Minetta Lane because that was where Gus Ricovic lived.

Remember Gus Ricovic? According to the *Daily News*, he had taken Gertie out for a date the night my Uncle Matt was murdered. Who he was beyond that the *Daily News* had not said, nor was it clear whether or not he had accompanied Gertie into the apartment and become a co-discoverer of the body, nor had there been any mention of him in any of the follow-up stories. But I wanted to know more about him, so when I'd gotten up this morning I'd looked him up in the phone book—everybody is in the phone book—and there he was, living on Minetta Lane.

The address was an old dark-brick apartment building, and

the name G. Ricovic was next to the bell-button for apartment 5-C. I rang, and waited, and had about decided nobody was home when all at once the door buzzer sounded. I leaped to the door and got it open just in time.

When I got to the fifth floor the door of apartment 5-C was standing open, showing a large square living room full of bad furniture from the Salvation Army. There was no one in sight. I stood tentatively in the doorway a second or two, and then tapped on the door.

A voice called, "Come on in!"

I entered, and the voice called, "Shut it, will ya?"

I shut it, and the voice called, "Take a seat."

I took a seat, and the voice was quiet.

To the right of where I was sitting, an arched doorway led to a long hall, this in semidarkness. From somewhere down there came the sound of running water, and the brisk scrub-scrub of someone brushing his teeth. This was followed by an interminable period of repulsive gargling sounds, and then a great deal of splashing—as though dolphins were at play nearby—and then what sounded like a towel repeatedly being snapped.

At last there was silence. I listened, and nothing seemed to be happening at all.

My mouth had become very dry. What was I doing here? What did I know about questioning people, about investigating murder cases, about unraveling complex schemes? Nothing. Less than nothing, in fact, because what little I did remember from my reading, I didn't know how to use.

I had come here to ask a man named Gus Ricovic some questions. What questions? And what did I hope to gain from his answers? If I asked him straight out if he was part of the gang that had killed Uncle Matt and kidnapped Gertie and shot at me, he would naturally say no, he wasn't. And what would that prove?

While trying to decide what it would prove, I looked up and saw someone coming down the dark hall toward me. At first I thought it was a young boy, and wondered why he was smoking a cigar, but then I realized he was an adult and merely unusually short.

He was wearing a white terrycloth robe, and he was barefoot, and yet the only word that possibly describes him is "dapper." A dapper little man with neat narrow feet, a neat narrow head, neat slicked-down black hair, neat tiny mustache, and a neat economy of movement. His right hand was in a pocket of his robe, in the manner of English nobility at the races, and with his left hand he removed the long and slender cigar from his mouth in order to say, "Don't believe I've had the pleasure, man."

"Fred Fitch," I said, getting to my feet. "Are you Gus Ricovic?"

"That's why I live here," he said, moving the cigar around like George Burns. "This is Gus Ricovic's pad, so this is where Gus Ricovic lives. What's a Fred Fitch?"

"I'm a friend of Gertie's," I said. "Also Matt Grierson's nephew."

"Ah, the money boy," he said, and smiled in Levantine pleasure. "Any friend of money is a friend of Gus Ricovic," he said. "Have you breakfasted?"

"Yes."

"Come watch," he said, and turned away.

I followed him into the dark hall and off to the right into an even darker kitchen. He hit a light-switch, nothing happened, and he said conversationally, "Have a seat, man. We talk while I ingest."

I couldn't see a thing. Did *he* think the light had gone on?

I stood in the doorway, trying to decide what to say and/or do, and all at once a furious flickering began all around me, with a white-on-white kitchen appearing and disappearing, like a midnight thunderstorm with lightning outside the windows.

But it was only a fluorescent ceiling fixture, somewhat more sluggish than most. It was pinging and buzzing up there, in time with its flickers, and with a final *zizzop!* it came completely on and stayed that way.

Gus Ricovic—for I supposed this was indeed he—was already at a cabinet across the way, reaching for a box of something called Instant Breakfast. "Fantastic invention," he commented, and took a paper packet out of the box.

Wondering if he meant fluorescent lighting, I pulled out one of the chrome-tube chairs by the formica table and sat down. "Yes, it is," I said, since comment seemed to be expected of me.

"The only breakfast that makes sense, man," he said, plunking the packet onto the counter beside the sink, so he hadn't meant the light after all. He went over to the refrigerator and got out a quart of milk. *En passant,* he said, "What's your will with me, pal?"

I said, "You were with Gertie the night my uncle was murdered."

"Ungood, man," he said, getting a glass from a cupboard. "Blood. Fuzz. Iron everywhere." He shuddered, and put the glass with the milk and the packet on the counter.

"You were in the apartment?"

"Wall-to-wall bluecoats," he said. "Looked like a civil rights meeting." He went over to another cupboard, opened it and got down a bottle of Hennessy brandy.

"Did you meet Gertie through Uncle Matt?" I asked, because it suddenly seemed important to know whose circle this odd little man had originally belonged to. I had no idea why it was important, but it seemed important, and so I asked.

Carrying the brandy to the counter, he said, "Nah, man. The other way around."

"You knew Gertie first."

He ripped open the packet. "Knew her for years," he said. "Buddy system." He shrugged.

"Would you mind telling me where you met her?"

He poured yellow powder from the packet into the glass. "Club in Brooklyn. We both worked there one time."

"You worked there?"

"Bongos, my friend," he said, and put down the packet, and drummed the counter a hot lick to demonstrate. "Strippers need bongos," he said, "like folk singers need guitars."

"Then you don't have any connection with my uncle."

He shrugged, and poured milk into the glass. "Got to know him some. Played him gin while the lady put her face on." He made dealing motions. "Dishonest old geezer, your uncle," he said.

"He cheated?"

"Not so's you couldn't notice it. Old and slow, man." He held his hands up close to his face and studied them as though they were recent acquisitions. "Someday these hands," he said, "will not know bongos. Hard to imagine."

"What did he say when you caught him?"

Ricovic shrugged, put his hands down, and used them to pour brandy in on top of the milk and the yellow powder. "A few dollars to make an old man happy," he said. "Besides, Gertie made good on it."

"You mean you let him get away with it."

He took a spoon from a drawer and began stirring the contents of the glass. "It's what Gertie wanted." He put the spoon down and faced me: "The question is, what do you want?"

"Information," I said.

"Information." He smiled slightly, picked up his glass, and said, "Follow."

We went back to the living room, where he motioned me back to the chair I'd been sitting in before, and then settled himself on the sofa. "Information," he repeated, seeming to enjoy the feel of the word in his mouth. "Like, vengeance is yours, is that how it goes?"

"I want to know who killed my uncle," I said. "For reasons of my own."

"Reasons of your own. You're a rich boy now."

"What's that got to do with anything?"

"When rich boys want information," he said, smiling at me, "all they have to do is wave money." He raised his glass in salute. "Your health," he said, and downed the whole glassful chugalug.

Carefully I said, "You mean *you* might know something?"

"I know the value of a dollar," he said. He put the empty glass on the coffee table, and wiped his mouth with the sleeve of his robe.

Was this for real, or was he trying to pull something, trying to peddle some cock-and-bull story made up out of his head? I said, "Naturally I'd pay a reward for information leading—"

"Yeah, yeah," he said. "Leading to the arrest and conviction of the guy that killed your uncle. I've read those cards, too."

"Well?"

"I tell you, man," he said, "my personal feeling is, there's many a slip twixt the arrest and the conviction. COD is not my style."

"You'd want your money beforehand."

"I'd feel safer that way."

I said, "Do you really have something to sell?"

He smiled. "Gus Ricovic," he said, "doesn't dicker for practice."

"The name of the killer?"

"That's the special of the week, my friend," he said.

"And proof," I said.

He shrugged. "Indications," he said. "I have the finger to point with, you have the eyes to see."

"I wouldn't want to give you money," I said, "for information I couldn't use."

"Fiscally sound, man. Maybe you shouldn't buy at all."

Damn him, he was in a seller's market and he knew it. He didn't care if I bought or not, or at least he could afford to act that way. I was the one approaching him, so the decision was up to me.

I said, "How much?"

"A thousand now," he said.

"Now?"

"Installment plan. Another thousand when the law puts the collar on the boy I name. And another thousand when he goes to trial, win or lose."

"Why so complicated?"

"Gus Ricovic has scruples," he told me. "If my information does nothing, it costs you one grand. If it helps, but not enough, it costs two grand. If it does the whole job, it costs three grand." He spread his hands. "Absolutely honest," he said.

I sat back to think about it, but I already knew I was going to do it. I said, "All right, I'll write you a check."

"Not hardly, my friend. You'll write me cash."

I could understand that, but I said, "I don't have a thousand dollars in cash."

"Who does? You take it out of your bank, you come back at six o'clock."

"Why six o'clock?"

"I'll need time to talk to the other party."

"What other party?"

"The party that did for your uncle. Naturally."

I didn't see anything naturally about it. I said, "You're going to *talk* to him?"

"You want some sort of unfair advantage? Naturally I have to give him the opportunity to meet your price."

"Meet my—! But you—you can't—*you're* the one—"

"Excuse me pointing this out, man," he said, "but you're sputtering."

"You're damn *right* I'm sputtering! What kind of—I'll come back here at six o'clock, you'll say oh, no, the price went up, the other party offered such and such, you'll have to pay at least so and so."

"Possibly," he said, judiciously granting me the point. "I tell you what we'll do, we'll limit it to two rounds of bidding. You play pinochle?"

"Pinochle?" I said.

"Two rounds of bidding? It's a phrase from pinochle."

I felt like a man with a wasp's nest in the attic of his skull. "What do I care?" I demanded. "Pinochle? What do you mean, pinochle? First you say you know something you'll sell, then you've got to talk to the other *party*, for God's sake, then it's two rounds of bidding, now it's pinochle. Maybe you don't know anything, what do you think of that? Maybe you're some kind of four-flusher, how does that grab you? That's a term from blackjack, it means you don't really have anything, you're bluffing." I got to my feet, driven upward in an excess of frustration. "I don't believe a word you've said," I told him, "and I wouldn't give you a thousand *cents*."

"Poker," he said.

"What?"

"Four-flush is a term from poker. It means you give the appearance of having five cards all in the same suit, but you only have four." He got to his feet. "I have five," he said. "And I'll see you at six o'clock."

"I knew that," I said. I pointed a finger at Gus Ricovic. "I *knew* it was poker. That's how upset you got me."

"My apologies, man," he said. "When you come back at six, I'll try not to increase the agitation."

TWENTY

Blackjack is a game where you're dealt two cards facedown, and if you want more cards they're dealt faceup, and the object of the game is to get as close as possible to twenty-one points—picture cards count ten—without getting more than twenty-one points. If at the end of the hand your cards come closer to twenty-one points than do the dealer's cards, you win.

Poker is a game where you're dealt five cards, and if you get one pair that's good but if you get two pair that's better, and three of a kind is better than that, and there are also straights and flushes and straight flushes and full houses and four of a kind.

I just want to point out that I did know all that. I don't know why I said four-flush was a term from blackjack. The only term from blackjack is *blackjack*.

Anyway, when I staggered out of Gus Ricovic's apartment I immediately took a cab back uptown to the bank, on my way to make the second withdrawal of the day.

Sitting in the back of the cab as slowly we progressed through New York's perpetual traffic snarl, I wondered if I was in the process of being played for a sucker yet a millionth time. Did Gus Ricovic really know who had killed Uncle Matt? If he did know, would he really tell me? If he did know and he really told me, would it ultimately do me any good?

In private-eye books, of which I've read my share, people are always buying information, and the information is always one hundred percent accurate. Nobody ever sells a private eye a lie, Lord knows why. But I wasn't a private eye, and Gus Ricovic might at this very moment be constructing for my special use a green and blue, six-sided, open-topped, reversible, large economy-size thousand-dollar whopper.

But I'd buy it, I knew that as well as he did. I had no idea how else to learn anything, and I might as well throw my money away at least *attempting* something.

But before you can throw money away you have to get your hands on it. Not always an easy thing to do, that, not if you've entrusted your money to a bank.

"Lot of money," said the teller dubiously, looking at the check I'd written and shoved across the counter to him.

"I'll take it in hundreds," I said.

"One moment," he said, and picked up his phone and checked my account. He seemed troubled by what he heard, put the phone down again, and studied my check with fretful eyes.

I said, "I have enough to cover it."

"Yes, of course," he said, not taking his eyes from the check. "Lot of money," he repeated.

"Hundreds," I repeated. "In a little envelope, if you have one."

"One moment," he repeated, and for a second I thought I was caught in a loop of time, endlessly backing on itself, circling around and around and around and never getting anywhere. But then, instead of picking up the phone and checking my account again, the teller walked away, carrying the check with him.

I leaned against the counter and waited. The woman behind me, Xmas Club booklet in hand, gave me a dirty look and went off to join another line.

The teller came back with another man, who was trying to look as dapper as Gus Ricovic but was failing. Of course, he had a gray suit on instead of a white terrycloth bathrobe, which may have made the difference. He smiled at me like a mechanical store-window Santa Claus and said, "Can I be of service?"

"You could cash my check," I said. "I'd like hundreds, if you have any."

The teller had already given this new one my check. The new one looked at it, seemed vaguely disturbed, and said, "Lot of money."

"Not really," I said. "Considering the national debt—"

He put my check on the counter and pointed over my shoulder. "I'm afraid you'll have to have this okayed," he said. "Mr. Kekkleman over there can help you, I'm sure."

"It's my money," I pointed out. "I'm just letting you people hold it for me."

"Yes, sir, naturally. Mr. Kekkleman will take care of everything for you."

So I went over to see Mr. Kekkleman, who sat at a desk behind an altar rail. He looked up at me with the bright expression of a man prepared instantly to make loans for solid collateral, and I said, "I need you to okay this check."

He took the check, looked at it, and his expression turned constipated. Before he could say it, I said, "Lot of money."

"Yes, it is," he said. "Would you have a seat?"

I sat down in the chair beside the desk. When he picked

up the phone I said, "The man over there already checked my account."

He gave me a blank distracted smile and checked my account. It took longer this time. I said, conversationally, "I'm thinking of taking all my money out of this stupid bank," and he gave me the same plastic smile.

Finally he put the phone down and said, "Yes, sir, Mr. Fitch. Would you give me a specimen signature?"

I burst out laughing.

His smile grew pained and puzzled. "Sir?"

"You just made me think," I told him, "about the specimens you have to give when you go see the doctor. You know, you take the little bottle into the men's room and all. And then I remembered a story I read once about some drunks who wrote their names in the snow that way. Specimen signatures, you see?"

He didn't think it was funny, and smiled so as to let me know it. Then he extended me a pen and a memo pad and I signed my name the old-fashioned way. He compared this signature with the one on the check, and this satisfied him. I have no idea why this satisfied him, since I'd written that check over on the other side of this same room not five minutes ago. Do crooks' signatures change every five minutes?

Well, I didn't make a fuss. He did some runes on the back of my check, I went over and stood in line behind the woman with the Xmas Club booklet, and in more time than it takes to tell about it I had ten hundred-dollar bills in a tiny manila envelope tucked away inside my wallet.

Free at last.

TWENTY-ONE

Dr. Osbertson's Park Avenue office was everything the Park Avenue office of a Park Avenue doctor should be, and his nurse blended in icy beauty with the décor.

I sat for a while in the waiting room with three dowagers. Then I sat for a while with two dowagers. Then I sat with one dowager. In the last stage I sat for a period of time alone. But at last the nurse held a door open and looked at me and said, "Mr. Nedick?"

I was afraid the name would make me blush, if I heard it too often. "Coming," I mumbled, and put down the copy of *Forbes* magazine I'd been leafing through—in some amazement, I might add—and followed her down a shiny corridor into a gleaming examination room, all white enamel and stainless steel.

"The doctor will be with you in just a moment," she said, and put a folder on a table, and went away, shutting the door behind her. The folder was empty, and on the tab was lettered very carefully in ink: *Nedick, F.*

Her idea of a moment was pretty unusual. It was two-thirty

when she left me in that room, and ten minutes to three—that's two-fifty, some people get confused—when Dr. Osbertson came briskly in, rubbing pudgy clean hands together and saying, "Well, now, what seems to be the trouble today?"

Seldom do people in real life resemble the fictional clichés erected to represent them, but Dr. Osbertson was the exception to the rule. He was fiftyish, distinguished, well padded, complacent and obviously well-off. He had the smile of an evil baby, and I swear I could feel his eyes undressing my wallet, though they seemed to miss the envelope full of hundreds.

I said, "Doctor, my name is Fitch. I'm—"

"What's this? The nurse has given me the wrong folder." He picked it up and started for the door with it.

"No, she didn't," I said. "I told her my name was Nedick. I didn't want you to know who I really was until I got here."

He stopped with one hand on the doorknob, the other clutching the empty folder, and looked at me with the attentive frown of a baby trying to understand why the watch ticks. Then he said, "I believe you've come to the wrong sort of physician. Mental disorders are not my—"

"Matthew Grierson was my uncle," I said.

He blinked at me, very slowly, and then said, "Ah, I see." He removed his hand from the doorknob, replaced the folder on the table, and smiled falsely at me, saying, "Well, this is a pleasure. Frankly, I don't understand—" He gestured at the folder.

"Some odd things have been happening," I said. "But they aren't important. The important thing is I want to talk to you about my uncle."

"Well, of course, his death wasn't from natural causes, was it? No, indeed. Actually, I should think the police would be the ones for you to talk to." He made a smallish movement toward the phone on the wall near the door. "Shall I call them for you?"

"I've already talked to them," I said. "Twice. Now I want to talk to you."

"Yes, of course." His smile had grown nervous, and he turned with some reluctance away from the phone. Whether this meant he had something to hide or merely thought he was dealing with a potential nut, I couldn't tell.

I said, "I understand my uncle had cancer."

"Yes, he did, that's right, that's what he had. Cancer." Osbertson was babbling, because of his nervousness, and he was looking around like a man who's lost something important and can't quite remember what it is.

I refused to be sidetracked. Hoping that calm and reasonable questioning would have a beneficial effect on him, so that sooner or later he'd settle down and begin to talk to me, I said, "I understand he'd had the cancer for several years."

"Yes, that's right. Six years, I believe, six years going on seven." He had drifted over to a side table and was fussily and distractedly moving things around on it: a little bottle, a tongue depressor, a package of disposable rubber gloves.

I said, "I understand he hadn't originally been expected to live this long."

"Oh, yes, that's true," he said forcefully, actually turning around to face me. "Very true," he said earnestly. "The original prognosis was death within a year. Within a year. Of course, that was a diagnostician in Brazil, but I myself was flown down not long afterwards and examined the subject and I must say I agreed with that diagnosis exactly. And other physicians since then have confirmed the diagnosis. Of course, there can't be any real precision in cases like this, the literature is full of cases of individuals who lived a greater or lesser time than was assumed in the diagnosis, and this man Grierson merely happened to be one of them. He could have gone at any moment. He would *not* have lived another six months, that I will state without equivocation. As to the general diagnosis in cases of this sort, no physician presumes to be offering an exact timetable, and the physician can't be blamed if the individual patient behaves in a manner differing from the norm."

Smiling, I said, "Well, I don't suppose Uncle Matt exactly *blamed* you for keeping him alive."

"Eh?" He'd been caught up in his explanation, and now all at once he seemed to remember whom he was talking to and what the subject was. "Oh, of course," he said. "Your uncle. Astonishing case, astonishing." With the return of memory had come the return of distraction; once again he was half-turned from me, pottering among the implements on his table.

I said, "You were his doctor for a long time, eh? I mean, even before he went to Brazil."

"What?" He touched a hypodermic syringe, a thermometer, a stethoscope. "Oh, no, not a bit. Never treated him till I went down to see him in Brazil. No, no, no previous history at all, not with me."

"I don't understand," I admitted. "How did he happen to pick you to come all the way to Brazil, if you'd never treated him before?"

He seemed startled. He put on a disposable rubber glove, took it off, disposed of it. "Mutual acquaintance, I suppose," he muttered, half-swallowing the words. "Some other patient."

"Who?"

"Couldn't say, couldn't possibly remember. Have to look it up in the records." He picked up the syringe, depressed the plunger, put it down. "Might not even be there."

"Well," I said, "I do want to talk to people who knew Uncle Matt. If it wouldn't be too much trouble, could you take a look and see if you do have it in the records?"

"Well, of course," he mumbled, "medical records, it's all confidential, not supposed to do that sort of thing." He picked up a bottle marked *Alcohol*, put it down. "Laymen," he said.

"I don't want to *see* anybody's records," I said. "If I could just know the name of the patient who recommended you to my uncle . . ."

He picked up a box of cotton pads, took out a pad, put the box down, put the pad down on the box. "Of course," he said indistinctly, talking into his chest, "those would be the old records, might be difficult to find . . ."

"If you'd look. Would you please look?"

"I'm not sure I'd—" He broke off, and turned even farther away from me. He picked up a small bottle, picked up the syringe, stuck the needle of the syringe through the stopper of the small bottle. He mumbled something I didn't catch, though the general rambling nature of it came through clearly enough.

What was he planning to do, inject me with something? Knock me out? Maybe even kill me. I backed farther away from him, looking around, and on a bench to my left I saw one of those little rubber hammers used by doctors to tap people on the knee. I edged closer to it.

Meanwhile, the doctor had raised his voice again, was saying, "All of this is most unorthodox, of course. Naturally, you understand a physician must be careful whom he deals with, who gets information and who does not. A physician has an obligation to his patients." And all the while he was drawing the fluid from the little bottle into the syringe, removing the needle from the bottle, putting the now-full syringe down on the table, discarding the bottle. He was obviously trying to keep me from noticing any of this, keeping his back to me, muttering away, trying to appear random and distracted.

I was close now to the rubber hammer. If he came toward me with that syringe I could get to the hammer in one leap.

With luck I'd knock the syringe from his hand and overpower him before he could do whatever he had in mind. I was his last patient of the day; if necessary I'd hold him prisoner here all night to get the information I wanted, and an explanation for his weird behavior.

In the interim, I was acting as though unaware of his preparations. I said, "You can understand my interest, I hope. After all, I did profit from my uncle's death, profited a great deal, and I feel a certain obligation to get to know him, even if it is only posthumously."

"Oh, naturally," he blathered. "Completely understandable, completely." As he spoke he was rolling up his left shirt sleeve. Was he trying to lull my suspicions, trying to make me think he was a diabetic or some such thing and preparing his normal injection?

He really went quite far with it, opening the alcohol bottle, wetting the cotton pad, cleaning a patch of skin on his inner left elbow. "Most natural instinct in the world," he nattered while doing this. "One feels a certain—kinship—to relatives who leave us money. Particularly a great deal of money. Oh, particularly."

He picked up the syringe.

I edged closer to the rubber hammer.

He stuck the needle in his arm and injected himself.

My mouth hung open like a sprung drawbridge. I watched him put the syringe down, place the cotton pad against the injection, bend his elbow, and turn at last away from the table. "I can understand your coming to see me," he said, still rambling, as he walked over to the paper-covered gray-leather examination table, sat down on it and then stretched out. "I'm sorry I can be of no real help to you," he said drowsily.

More loudly than I'd expected, I shouted, "What have you done?"

"One hundred," he said. "Ninety-nine. Ninety-eight. Ninety-seven."

I raced over to him. His eyes were closed, his features relaxed, his hands crossed on his chest. He looked very peaceful. "Wake up!" I shouted. "You've got to answer my questions! Wake up!"

"Ninety-six," he said. "Ninety-fi. Nine-four. Ni-th. Ni. Nnnnnnn."

I shook him. I slapped his cheeks. I screamed in his ear. I half-climbed atop him, straddling him with one leg the better to grasp his shoulders and shake him, and I was in that position when the door opened and the nurse came in.

She screamed. She shrieked, "Murder!" She went tearing away down the corridor, screaming. "He's murdered the doctor!"

Dr. Osbertson slept on, faintly smiling. As for me, I fled.

TWENTY-TWO

My return home bore a marked similarity to Napoleon's departure from Russia. I had gone out with a head full of grand plans and predetermined goals, and I was coming back without my army. As for my six o'clock appointment with Gus Ricovic, I did not right now have very high hopes.

I approached my block circumspectly, but once again there was no sign of my would-be assassins. With one last quick look around, I ducked into my doorway.

The mailbox was full again. I emptied it into my pockets and went on upstairs.

For once there was no one to greet me at my door, not even Wilkins. I went inside, emptied the mail from my pockets to the table near the door, and went out to the kitchen to prepare myself one of the first pre-sundown drinks of my life.

If I had ever thought there was any chance of my being a detective, I now knew better. I'd gone out to question two men, and one of them had put himself to sleep rather than answer me. Unconscious, he had routed me.

Of course, it might be construed as progress of a kind. After all, Dr. Osbertson wouldn't have knocked himself out if he hadn't had something to hide, would he?

I considered briefly the notion that Dr. Osbertson had murdered Uncle Matt himself, in a fit of pique at Uncle Matt's having proved his diagnosis to be so completely off the beam. To a professional man, it might seem a sort of insult to say a man will die in a year and then have the man live *five* years beyond the diagnosis. If Uncle Matt hadn't been hit on the head with a blunt instrument he might have outlived his physician.

But that was a fairly silly reason for murder. No, it wouldn't do. The murder had something to do with money, the money I'd inherited. There was no reason for any of the rest of this, otherwise.

So what was Dr. Osbertson hiding? The identity of the patient who had recommended him to Uncle Matt? But why would that be something worth hiding?

The extent of my ignorance in this sea of occurrences sometimes startled me and sometimes disheartened me. At the moment it was doing both.

How could I find out what Dr. Osbertson knew and didn't want me to know? If I went back to see him again, God alone knew what he might do. Shoot himself in the foot. Operate on his vocal cords. Inject himself with German measles and put himself in quarantine.

My first drink didn't solve any problems, so I had a second. As I sipped at it, I dialed Gertie's number on the off-chance, but there wasn't any answer. I then went through today's in-pouring of mail and found it—with one exception—to be another dose of yesterday's avalanche. I threw the rest away and took a closer look at my exception.

It was a plain envelope, with no name or address or any other writing on it. Nor a stamp; it hadn't been mailed but had been dropped into my mailbox by someone while I was out.

Inside was a small sheet of stationery, folded once. I opened it up and found a typed message inside, short and sweet. It read:

> Call me.
> Professor Kilroy
> CH2-2598

Professor Kilroy. Where had I heard that name before? Somewhere . . .

Gertie. She'd said Professor Kilroy was my Uncle Matt's partner down in Brazil!

Maybe at last I'd start finding out what was going on!

I had the number almost all dialed when caution suddenly reasserted itself. This was a Chelsea number, which meant somewhere in this neighborhood. The note claimed to be from Professor Kilroy, but what if it wasn't? What if it was a trick, to get me to announce when I was home? The gang could be a block from here, three buildings from here, just waiting for the phone to ring.

No, the thing to do was get out of the neighborhood, get uptown, and call from there. And for once in my life I was going to *do* the thing that was the thing to do. Back on went my coat, into my pocket went Professor Kilroy's note, and out the door went I.

Twenty-Three

I knew just the place to go: the newspaper library. At least when I began to read a newspaper it didn't put itself to sleep on me or start auctioning its information. And it had occurred to me that some of the characters in this cast of thousands might from time to time have been newsworthy. Professor Kilroy, for instance. Or Uncle Matt. Or Gus Ricovic. Anything I found out about their past activities might be of help to me.

Or, on the other hand, it might not.

In any case, it seemed best to leave the apartment, and the newspaper library was as good a place to go as any, and better than some. So I left my snug lair once again, and as I hurried away toward Eighth Avenue, I found myself amazed at the neighborhood's continued lack of assassins. It seemed I'd just managed to double-think them somehow; I was a sort of living purloined letter, hidden in the most obvious place and therefore unseeable.

It was twenty past three when I arrived at the library. By five o'clock, when I left, I'd learned a little but I'd also run across some surprising blanks. Professor Kilroy, for example, hadn't appeared at all, nor—except for his murder—had my Uncle Matt. Reilly had showed up a few times, in connection with Bunco Squad arrests, but Karen Smith had never appeared at all. Wilkins had appeared once, having something obscure to do with the 1949 Berlin airlift. Mr. Grant had never made the *Times.* I'd expected Goodkind to be in constantly, but he appeared only once, when a former client for whom he had successfully prosecuted a damage suit against a large elevator corporation turned around and sued him for having kept over half the proceeds. Neither Gertie nor Gus Ricovic appeared, but Dr. Lucius Osbertson did, just once. Seven years ago he'd been the physician for a man named Walter J. Cosgrove, a financier whose testimony was wanted in a fraudulent stock deal. Dr. Osbertson had sworn his client was too ill to testify at that time. I looked up Cosgrove, and discovered that three days after Dr. Osbertson's testimony Cosgrove escaped to Brazil, taking with him, in the newspaper's estimation, "upwards of two million dollars in cash and negotiable securities." I've never been sure whether *upwards of* means *more than* or *almost,* but I got the general idea.

Cosgrove's departure for Brazil took place a year after Uncle Matt's, and two years before Uncle Matt's return. I wondered if Cosgrove and Uncle Matt had gotten to know one another down there in Brazil, if it was Cosgrove who had called Osbertson down to see to Uncle Matt when Uncle Matt had fallen ill.

I wondered if any of the money Uncle Matt had brought back had at one time belonged to Walter J. Cosgrove.

It seemed to me likely that the name Cosgrove was what Dr. Osbertson had been hiding this afternoon; he was probably still trying to live down the blot to his reputation. But if that was all it was, his action seemed a little extreme. No, there was still more to this than I understood.

When I left the newspaper library, I walked over to the gas station at Tenth Avenue and 42nd Street and used the phone booth there. I dialed the number on Professor Kilroy's note, and it was answered after three rings by a gravelly voice saying, "Yes? What is it?"

"Professor Kilroy, please," I said. The name sounded as foolish in its way as did Fred Nedick, but I didn't feel as silly pronouncing it; I wasn't Professor Kilroy.

The gravelly voice said, "Who is this?"

"Fred Fitch," I said. "Is this Professor Kilroy?"

"Where are you? You to home?"

"Never mind where I am. Is this Professor Kilroy?"

"Sure. Who do you think it is? You think I give you somebody else's number? Where you want to meet, your place or mine?"

"Neither," I said, I'd thought about this part of it, and had finally decided on the safest place to meet this man, whoever he was. "I'll meet you," I said, "at Grand Central, the main waiting room."

"How come?"

"I have no way to be sure who you are."

"Listen, kid, all I'm doing is helping out the nephew of an old pal, that's my only interest in this."

"My only interest," I told him, "is protecting myself. I'll meet you at Grand Central or nowhere."

"Sure, what the hell, Grand Central. Any special time?"

"I'll leave that up to you."

"Eight o'clock, okay? After the rush hour."

"All right by me," I said. "How will I recognize you?"

"Don't worry," he said. "I'll recognize you."

Click.

Twenty-Four

Now for Uncle Matt's apartment.

I had waited this long to go there because I was fairly certain that Goodkind would be spending at least part of today hanging around its vicinity in hopes of getting my ear for a fast lesson in hypnosis. I had no idea what his role in all this might be, whether he was connected with the murderer/kidnappers or if he had some separate plot of his own afoot, but I did know enough about my own gullibility and I had seen enough of his smiling face to know that my only safety lay in avoiding him.

But he couldn't stake out Uncle Matt's apartment forever. Sooner or later he would have to give it up, called away by the pressure of his business. Surely by now he had to be somewhere suborning a jury, or foreclosing on a widow, or pursuing an ambulance. Hoping this assumption was correct, I sidled under cover of the rush hour up to that part of West 59th Street known as Central Park South, found the right building, and lurked around until I was fairly certain Attorney Goodkind was nowhere in the vicinity. Then I approached the doorman, who looked mainly like an admiral in the Bolivian Navy.

At first he pretended I wasn't there, as I'm sure he fervently wished. I suppose I just didn't look the Central Park South type, and I assume he thought me a tourist, wanting him to point out to me the passing celebrities: Killer Joe Piro, Barbra Streisand, General Hershey.

When I finally took the tactic of standing directly in front of him and obstructing his attempt to flag cabs, he reluctantly acknowledged my existence by giving me an impatient, "Yes? What is it?"

"The keys to the Grierson apartment," I said.

If I'd expected any sudden change in manner, any abrupt shift to bowing and scraping, I was to be disappointed. With the same gruff impatience, he reached into the trouser pocket of his admiral's uniform, produced two keys attached by a bit of dirty string to a round red tag, and handed it to me without a word or a look. Then he stepped around me and blew his whistle violently at the world.

Inside, I was stopped by another naval officer, this one a mere commander in the Swiss Maritime, who with barely concealed hostility wanted to know who it was I hoped to see.

"Nobody," I said. "I own an apartment in this building. The Matthew Grierson apartment."

This time there was a change, to a rather offensive sort of chumminess. The commander said, "Oh, yeah? You inherited, huh? Rags to riches, huh?"

How was it that people like this instinctively knew they could get away with such treatment of me? Money isn't everything, a fact of which rotters like this one were endlessly eager to remind me.

I said, "Not exactly," knowing it to be a weak response, and went on by him and across the long low-ceilinged lobby to the elevators. I told the operator, "The Grierson apartment," he slid his doors shut, and up we went.

On the way, the operator—green uniform, possibly a passed-over captain in the Merry Men Brigade—said, "You the nephew?"

Not another one. With a sinking heart I said, "Yes, I am."

But he wasn't exactly another one. He was simply the garrulous type. "Mr. Grierson used to talk about you a lot," he said. He was a gnarled and weatherbeaten man of about fifty, thin and somewhat stoop-shouldered. "We used to play cards together sometimes," he went on, "when my tour was done. Sometimes he'd be reading a report on you."

"Is that right?"

"Yes, sir," he said. "My favorite tenant, your uncle. Never uppity, like a lot of these people. Paid his debts, too, on the button. If he'd lose, he'd write you a check right then and there."

"Did he lose a lot?" I asked, wondering if this little man had been picking my uncle in a small-time way.

But he said, "No, sir, he mostly won. He was real lucky, your uncle."

It seemed as though that last had been said with some kind of an edge in the voice, but I couldn't be sure, and before I could say anything more the elevator came to a stop, the doors opened, and he was pointing away to the left, saying, "That's it there, sir, 14-C. It's really the thirteenth floor, but most people are superstitious, you know? So they call it fourteen."

"That's interesting," I said, as I stepped out of the elevator.

"But it's still the thirteenth floor," he said. "Ain't that so? You go outside and count the windows, this here's the thirteenth floor, ain't it?"

"I suppose it is," I said.

"Sure it is," he said. Then he shook his head, said, "Rich people," shut his doors, and went away.

It took two keys on two locks to get into Uncle Matt's

apartment, which had the musty smell of disuse and which, when I began switching on lights, sprang into existence like a series of no-longer-needed movie sets.

The style represented here was surely not Uncle Matt's, not from all I'd heard about the old man. Undoubtedly the building itself had an interior decorator on tap who had designed and furnished this apartment. It was the sort of thing Uncle Matt would more than likely leave to someone else to take care of; I doubted he cared very much what his surroundings looked like, so long as they sufficiently had the appropriate smell of money.

The rooms went on and on. A long broad living room on two levels, with a lot of long low sofas and on the walls long abstract paintings, and great drape-flanked windows at the end giving a beautiful long view of Central Park. Following a curve of wrought-iron railing away from all this grandeur, one came to a small formal dining room with dark red fabric wall covering and heavy wood antique furnishings. A shiny white compact but very complete kitchen was off this, through a swinging door with a porthole in it.

Away from the dining room in the other direction one came to a game room, with a pool table *and* a poker table, the latter with chip trays and glass holders. Past this were two large elaborate bedrooms, both with canopied king-size beds and outsize views of Central Park. Each bedroom had its own Pompeiian bathroom, in one of which was a sauna. Beyond the second bedroom was a sort of den or office, with a desk and with built-in bookshelves containing books I'm sure no one had ever read. And off in yet another direction was a smallish plain bedroom with its own attached prim bath; servant's quarters, no doubt.

Uncle Matt had done well for himself. He'd spent his declining years in comfort.

I wandered around the rooms, not sure what I was looking for and not sure what I was finding. If it was Uncle Matt's personality, some aura of him, I had hoped to find here, I doubted I was getting it. The dominant personality here was the interior decorator's. Other than that, I suppose I mostly just wanted to take a look at the scene of the crime.

Which was the game room. Uncle Matt had been found, according to the text and photo in the *Daily News*, facedown in the game room, between the pool table and the poker table. A pool game had been in progress, with only one cue out, so it was assumed Uncle Matt had been shooting a solitary game of pool when he'd been struck down.

I stood looking at the very spot on the carpet for a while, learned nothing, theorized nothing, and finally went away to wander through the other rooms, getting nowhere until I settled down at the desk in the office.

Then I'm not sure where I got. I found a few odd pieces of stationery here and there, letters from this person and that, nothing very enlightening. There was a bill from Goodkind, with an ingratiating, palsy-walsy, yet obsequious letter accompanying it that made me think most of Uriah Heep. There was a letter from another attorney, a Prescott Wilks, taking exception to Uncle Matt's having done with the service of his firm, and one paragraph of this letter struck me as a little odd:

> You know the circumstances as well as I, Mr. Grierson, and I needn't tell you our mutual friend is as upset as I am at this abrupt and unjustifiable termination of your relationship with this firm. I have been asked to communicate to you the information that any alteration in the arrangements or any plans you might have for "striking out on your own," as it were, will not be treated

lightly. Kindly bear this in mind in your future dealings
with Latham, Courtney, Wilks & Wilks.

Apparently there had been no future dealings with Latham,
Courtney, Wilks & Wilks; the letter was dated four months
ago, there was no more recent correspondence that I could see,
and Goodkind seemed securely in control of the situation by
the time I had entered the affair.

What interested me was the veiled threat I seemed to dis-
tinguish in that one paragraph of Wilks' letter. Who was the
mutual friend? What sort of relationship had Uncle Matt had
with Prescott Wilks' firm? What exactly did the phrase "will
not be treated lightly" mean? Did it mean murder?

I was bothered a bit by the knowledge that surely Steve
and Ralph had seen this letter and had investigated its meaning, but against this fact I put the uncertainty I felt about Steve
and Ralph, who might have sold out to the gang, who might
have been the ones to tell the gang where I was hiding, and
who might be covering for the murderers instead of seeking
them out. After all, as Gertie had said, nobody was likely to
accuse Steve and Ralph of being priests.

Thinking of Gertie, I decided to try her apartment again,
but when I picked up the phone the line was dead. Goodkind
must have seen to cutting off the service, which was very alert
and thrifty of him, but with three hundred thousand dollars I
could surely afford to keep the phone going in my other apartment.

Would I live here? Somehow I thought not; the place was
too much like the lobby of Radio City Music Hall. I'd keep
expecting tourist groups to be led through by guides. Besides,
I couldn't spend my entire life being cowed by doormen. No, I'd
have Goodkind put the place up for sale. All in all, I thought
I'd stay in my own place on West 19th Street. I'd never found

it less than satisfactory before, so why should I change it now?

Ah, but that was in the future, when all this mess was over and I could lead my normal life again. As to now, I was allegedly investigating Uncle Matt's apartment, for reason or reasons unknown. Therefore I copied the address of Latham, Courtney, Wilks & Wilks from the letter onto a piece of scrap paper, tucked the paper into my pocket, and went on with my search.

I made my next discovery in the closet off the maid's bedroom. That's where I found the crumpled-up body of Gus Ricovic.

TWENTY-FIVE

At first I didn't realize he was dead. He was sitting on the floor, knees up, back against the wall, chin on knees, all tucked in the corner. His eyes were open, wide open, and on his face he had a sort of bland and faintly quizzical smile. He appeared to be looking at my ankles, and all in all the naturalness of his expression and posture had me absolutely fooled for perhaps ten seconds, during which time I was (a) amazed and (b) cynical.

I was (a) amazed because who wouldn't be, opening a closet door and finding Gus Ricovic tucked away on the floor inside? And I was (b) cynical because the immediate explanation for his presence which came to me was, "Oh ho! He's come looking for something to sell." That is, in the instant of seeing him I leaped to the assumption that when he had offered to sell me information he had actually been possessed of no information to sell and had therefore come rushing over here to see if by some rare stroke of luck he might find some information I'd later be willing to buy. This thought took much less time to think than it does to describe.

In any case, it very quickly became superseded by (c) horror. That was when I noticed that Gus Ricovic wasn't moving, his eyes weren't blinking, and there seemed to be something stickily wrong with the top of his head. "Oh," I said, and slammed the door.

Then the noise of the slam scared me. Was the killer still somewhere close by? Had I spent the last half-hour playing hide and seek, all unknowing, with a multiple murderer? And now that I had found the latest body, would this murderer think it necessary to add me to his collection?

No, that couldn't be right. Whoever had killed Uncle Matt was already out to kill me and had made his intentions perfectly plain. And could there be any doubt that the same Mister X had done for Gus Ricovic? Whether Ricovic had come here hoping to find information to sell, or whether he had been killed as a result of trying to blackmail the killer, there was still no doubt that the same murdering hand had clubbed down both Uncle Matt and the thing in the closet.

So I had to be alone in the apartment, just me and Gus Ricovic. I didn't open the closet door any more, I already knew what he looked like. I turned my back, started walking, and three rooms later my brain at last caught up with me.

The first thing my brain wanted to know was, What now? Call the police? No, for the same reasons that I hadn't called them when Gertie was kidnapped. In fact, I could handle this the same way, getting to the safe ground of a neutral phone booth somewhere. Aside from its other advantages, this plan had the admirable feature of getting me out of this apartment, in which the air suddenly seemed to have gotten both damp and chilly. Clammy. Like a mausoleum.

Gus Ricovic's body seemed to vibrate way back in its dark closet at the far end of the apartment. As though invisible strings were attached to it, leading to every other room, the air seemed to ring and echo with his presence. It was like being in a cave inside an iceberg, with something rotting off in a corner.

Anyway, it was time for my meeting with Professor Kilroy.

I left the apartment at a fast walk, fumbled with the keys as I locked the door, and even with that door between us, still felt the clammy tendrils of Gus Ricovic trailing along the back of my neck. I shivered, and pushed the button for the elevator.

My friendly elevator operator arrived, not soon enough, and as soon as I boarded he turned a worried face to me and said, "I been thinking about things, Mr. Grierson."

"Fitch," I said, distracted. I was thinking that I had never seen a dead body before and would prefer never to see a dead body again. Ever. Particularly not in closets in empty apartments.

"Yeah, that's right," the operator was saying. "I remember. Mr. Grierson explained me that one time, how you had different names."

"Did he?" I said.

"Mr. Fitch," he said urgently, "I hope you won't say nothing to the management here about me playing cards with your uncle or anything like that. We're not supposed to mingle with the tenants, you know. I mean, I wouldn't of done it if your uncle hadn't wanted me to."

"I won't say anything," I said.

"It could cost me my job," he said. "I wouldn't know what to do without this job."

I said nothing to that, having problems of my own to think about, and when at last the elevator doors opened on the ground floor I went away without reassuring him any more about his tenure. Besides, hadn't he heard of self-service elevators? Sooner or later automation must spread even to Central

Park South, whether I finked on his chumming with Uncle Matt or not.

I wondered how the Bolivian admiral out front had liked having Uncle Matt for a tenant.

I wondered how I could manage so many irrelevant thoughts with Gus Ricovic sitting up there in that dark closet.

Three blocks from the apartment building I found an outdoor phone booth. Being wise in the ways of the Police Department by now, I succeeded in anonymously reporting the body in the closet in under five minutes, having run through the inevitable battery of Sergeant Sreeses and Tective Sreeses and Friggum-Steen Precincts like Roger Bannister through the four-minute mile.

As I was coming out of the phone booth, it occurred to me to wonder by how narrow a margin had I missed the murderer or murderers of Gus Ricovic. Had they left half an hour before I'd come? Or five minutes? Or thirty seconds?

Had they perhaps been going down in one elevator while I was going up in the other?

It was almost time to go meet Professor Kilroy, but the growing realization of how close perhaps I had come to taking the long walk hand in hand with Gus Ricovic made a preliminary stop necessary.

There was the place, just down the block, its door under the red neon sign that said BAR.

TWENTY-SIX

I had about decided he wouldn't show up. It was ten minutes past eight, the cavernous interior of Grand Central was sparsely populated. I sat on a bench where I could watch most of the great room, waiting to see any familiar face, any one at all. I would flee as though pursued by demons, which I might as well be. I could still remember, only too clearly, having been shot at not so very long ago. Not to mention the quizzical smile and unblinking eyes of Gus Ricovic.

But the man who emerged out of nowhere and plopped down onto the bench beside me was no one I had ever seen before in my life. He had a great scraggly bushy black beard with great streaks of gray in it, his hair was long and unkempt and also black with streaks of gray, his face seemed to be just slightly dirty, and he wore great thick spectacles with horn rims, the right wing of which was broken and haphazardly fixed with Scotch tape. He was of medium height, but dressed in an old tweed suit a good two or three sizes too large for him. His shirt was also too large for him, and his orange-and-red tie was put together with the largest knot I'd seen in years, the sort of knot we used to call a Windsor when it was sported by all the sharpest blades in high school.

"Hello, kid," he said, in the most gravelly voice I ever heard in my life, "I'm Professor Kilroy."

I said, "I guess you already know who I am."

"Sure," he said. "Short Sheet pointed you out to me one time."

"Short—? Oh, you mean Uncle Matt."

"Matt, yeah." He wiped the back of his hand across his mouth and looked vaguely out around the terminal. "Let's go someplace and get a drink," he said.

"I'd rather stay right here," I told him.

"Yeah," he said. He squinted at me through his glasses. "You gone paranoid, huh?"

"If you mean I've finally learned you can't trust anybody, you're right."

"Smart kid," he said. "I figured no nephew of Matt's could be one hundred percent shlemiel."

I wondered what percent shlemiel he figured I was, but I said, "You wanted to talk to me about something."

"Yeah, that's right." He wiped his mouth again, glanced out around the terminal some more, and said, "I could do with a drink, you know? I'm kinda nervous, to be seen with you."

That made *me* nervous. I looked quickly around, saw no one with a machine gun, and said, "Why should you be nervous?"

"I don't want 'em mad at me anymore."

"Who?"

"The Coppo boys."

"The who?"

He looked at me. "You don't know nothing about nothing, do you?"

"I never heard of the Coppo boys," I said.

"Where do you think all that dough came from?"

"I don't know. From Brazil somewhere."

"That's right. From Pedro Coppo."

"He's one of the Coppo boys?"

He shook his head. "Naw. He was their father."

"Was?"

"Lemme start at the beginning, will ya?" he asked me.

"Sure," I said.

"You heard of Brasilia, right?"

"I think so. It's a new city."

"Right. Started about ten years ago, in the back country, way the hell away from anywhere. There was a lot of money made there, kid, a lot of money. Me, I operated a little store there myself for a while, down in the workers' part. Shack City, you know?"

"A store?"

He made dealing motions. "Cards," he said. "Like that. They love to gamble, those South Americans. It's the hot Latin blood."

"Did Uncle Matt have a store there, too?"

"For a while. We known each other for years, sometimes we put in with each other, sometimes we work single-o. You know what I mean?"

"I think so," I said.

"So there was this bird Coppo," Professor Kilroy said. "Pedro Coppo. He was one of the boys cleaning up there in Brasilia. Construction, you know? Trucking. Trucking companies made a fortune. Coppo was in all over the place, finger in this pie, finger in that pie." He demonstrated with downward jabbing motions.

"I've got it," I said.

"So Short Sheet had him a con figured, a really sweet con. Complicated, you know? Land tracts and like that. He needed somebody to be a surveyor from General Motors, so I stood in. He took that Coppo for almost a million bucks." He waved his hands around in remembered excitement. "I got a hundred grand for myself," he said, "and Short Sheet got the rest. He went to Rio and had himself a time."

Trying a long shot, I said, "Is that where he met Walter Cosgrove?" Because Walter Cosgrove was the only other patient of Dr. Lucius Osbertson that I knew of, and he and Uncle Matt had been in Brazil at the same time.

Professor Kilroy looked startled, then began briskly to wipe his mouth and scratch inside his coat. "Cosgrove?" he asked me. "Who's Cosgrove?"

"It doesn't matter," I said. I was convinced Professor Kilroy knew who Walter Cosgrove was, but I didn't see any point in pressing the issue. I didn't want to scare him away before he'd finished telling me the part he was willing to talk about. So I said, "What happened next? After Uncle Matt went to Rio?"

"What happened next," he said, "is Pedro Coppo killed himself. Who would of thought it? He was a smart type, he could of made himself another million easy. But out a window he went, right there in Brasilia. To show you how new everything was then, he landed in wet cement."

"Oh," I said. "In other words, I've inherited blood money."

"There's a lot of blood on that dough, by now," he said. "Pedro Coppo. Short Sheet. Almost me, and maybe you."

And Gus Ricovic, but there was no point my mentioning that.

"The Coppo boys," I said, beginning to understand. "The sons. They're out to revenge their father."

"You got it," he said. He looked around nervously. "And they're rough boys. Two of them, twin brothers."

"They're here in the States?"

"They been here for years," he said. "They come up here

long before their old man went out the window." He leaned closer to me and whispered harshly, "They're in the rackets. They got the whole mob behind them."

"Then they're the ones that killed my uncle."

"Or ordered it done," he said. "They're big boys now, they don't have to do the rough stuff themselves. All they do is point, and you're dead."

I was thinking of the shots from the moving car. That was gangland style, certainly. What sort of inheritance was this, that came with professional killers attached?

Professor Kilroy was wiping his mouth continually now, and looking more and more agitated. It was no surprise at all when he said, "Kid, I'm sorry, but I need a drink. Will you come with me?"

"I'd rather not," I said. "I feel safer here, in the open."

"You aren't safe anywhere, kid," he said. "That's the point I'm trying to get across." He wiped his mouth so vigorously he almost knocked his glasses off. "I really need that drink," he said. "I tell you what, you wait here and I'll be right back."

"I don't like that either," I said.

"You think I'm going to sell you out, call somebody and say here he is? I didn't have to show up at all if that's what I had in mind."

That was true enough. I said, "All right. I'll wait ten minutes, no more."

"It's a deal." He sprang to his feet, then hesitated, hanging over me, and said, "You wouldn't have a dollar on you."

"A dollar?"

"I told you a lot already," he said, "and I got a lot more to tell you. It's worth a dollar. It's worth a lot more than a dollar."

I took out my wallet, found a dollar bill, and handed it to him. It disappeared at once somewhere within his outsize clothing, and away he shambled, with a funny rushing sort of limp, scrabbling across the terminal floor like some weird bird, reminding me most of Emmett Kelly all made up in his sad-clown costume.

While he was gone I sat and thought over what he'd so far told me. It was all beginning to make sense now; Uncle Matt's mysterious acquisition of riches in Brazil, his murder, the try at killing me, the kidnapping of Gertie. That too was gangland style. I suppose they thought Gertie might know where I was, or maybe they were holding her for ransom and sooner or later I'd be hearing from them.

That presented a problem. If they did find me, what crime would they have in mind, extortion or murder? If murder, my job was to cut and run. If extortion, if they wanted me to pay for Gertie's release, of course I would.

I determined to ask Professor Kilroy about Gertie when he came back.

But would he come back? I looked at my watch and eight minutes had gone by. I was beginning to get a little nervous. Or, that is, I had already been a little nervous and I was now getting a little *more* nervous.

It's astonishing how many people look like members of the mob, if you look at them closely. Carrying suitcases full of bombs, carrying overcoats slung over their arms to hide sawed-off shotguns. There were even three tough-looking guys carrying violin cases.

Professor Kilroy *had* sold me out, I was suddenly sure of it. His ten minutes had wound themselves out and he wasn't here. The terminal was filling up with professional killers, slowly closing in on me.

I got to my feet, dithering, not knowing which way to turn, and finally just walked briskly off to the nearest rank of lockers. I stood half out of sight behind these and watched the bench I had just left.

Nothing happened.

Nothing happened for one hundred and eighty seconds. I thought I might make a dash for the door. On the other hand, that might be exactly what they were waiting for.

But could they guard all the doors? What if I went out onto the platform and around and out to the taxi stand? Or was there someone out on the platform waiting to throw me onto the third rail?

Professor Kilroy appeared, hurrying, and scrambled over to the bench where we'd been sitting. He stood there in obvious perplexity, looking around and seeming very agitated. There was no one with him.

Still hesitant, I came out from behind the lockers and walked slowly over to rejoin the Professor. He saw me coming and rushed over to me, saying, "What happened? You see one of them?"

"I'm not sure," I said. "I guess not." I sat down again where I'd been.

He stayed on his feet, very agitated, looking all around. "Maybe we oughta get outa here," he said.

"No. I feel safe here."

"It's bad to stay in one place too long."

"Sit down," I said. "Tell me the rest. There can't be much more."

"There ain't." He sat down, but he was still very nervous, moving his hands and feet a lot. "After the old man kicked off," he said, "his sons swore to get us. Matt and me. They caught up with me three years ago."

"They didn't kill you," I pointed out.

"They knew I was small potatoes," he said. "They knew Short Sheet was the artist on that one. I give 'em back all the money I had left, they roughed me up a little, and that was it.

They wouldn't even of roughed me up, but they thought I knew where Short Sheet was."

"You didn't?"

He winked, and leaned closer, and whispered, "I did, but I conned them. I wouldn't sell out an old pal." I could smell whiskey on his breath.

I said, "But they did kill Uncle Matt."

"Because he was the brains. And because he wouldn't give 'em back the dough. At least, that's what I figure. I figure it took 'em all this time to find him 'cause they couldn't believe he'd be right here under their noses in New York City, and of course they didn't know his real name. But they found him finally. They kept on looking till they did."

"And now they're after me," I said.

"They're after the money," he said. "They don't care about you, any more than they cared about me. Less, you didn't have nothing to do with the con. But they don't like the idea anybody getting the advantage of that money. That's why they made me give it back." He wiped his mouth and said, "I shouldn't of done it. You know what I should of done?"

"What?"

"I should of give it to some charity," he said. "Some orphanage or something."

"But wouldn't they have killed you if they didn't get the money back?"

"What do they care about the money? They got all the dough they need. It's just they didn't want me getting the benefit." Bitterly, he added, "And I shouldn't of let *them* get the benefit."

I said, "I think they kidnapped a friend of mine. Maybe you know her, Gertie Divine. She lived with my uncle."

He squinted at me. "The stripper? They kidnapped her?"

"What do you suppose? Do they want to kill me, or do they want me to pay ransom for her?"

"Did she inherit anything?"

"Not that I know of," I said. "I think I was the only one inherited anything."

"Don't count on it," he said. "That wouldn't be like Short Sheet, leave his pal Gertie out in the cold. He seen to it she got something, don't you worry."

"You think that's why they kidnapped her?"

"Sure. Squeeze the dough out of her, what else? Why ask you to pay ransom for her? She ain't your kid."

"I thought that might be what they had in mind," I said.

"You worry about yourself, kid," he said, and patted my knee. "You got plenty to worry about right there, believe you me."

"I believe you," I said.

He said, "Listen, what was that name you brought up before? Cosgrove?"

"Walter Cosgrove."

"Yeah. That name's got like a familiar ring to it. Who is he?"

"Nobody important," I said. I had the feeling Professor Kilroy had it in his mind to pump me about Walter Cosgrove, to find out how much I knew about the man and where I'd gotten my information, and something—I suppose what the Professor had termed paranoia—told me that any knowledge I could keep to myself was nothing but points for my side.

He persisted though, saying, "I feel like I know the name from somewhere is all. Walter Cosgrove. What is he, another grifter?"

"It doesn't matter," I said. "What do you think I ought to do about the Coppo brothers? Go to the police?"

"Listen," he said, "those boys already got half the cops in

the city on their payroll, just in the normal line of business. You go to a cop, how do you know he isn't somebody'll turn you right over to the Coppos?"

"I was thinking that myself," I said gloomily. "In fact, I'd suspected there might be some crooked police involved in this somewhere."

"You think there's any other reason they never solved your uncle's murder?"

"I guess not."

"Some of these amateur outfits," he said, "like kak and the Crime Commission, they do pretty good work sometimes, but there ain't enough of them. The cops still have it all their own way."

"So what should I do?"

"If you think you can disappear," he said, "go ahead and do it. If not, my advice is unload that inheritance. Turn it all over to some charity, every bit of it. And do it loud and clear, with your picture in the papers and everything. Just so they know."

"But," I said, "all that money."

"It'll never bring you nothing but grief, kid," he said. "You called it yourself. Blood money, you said, and that's what it is. Two men are dead already for that money. Maybe Short Sheet's stripper is dead too, by now. And maybe you'll be dead in a couple days. I don't know how you kept away from them so long already. Beginner's luck maybe."

"Maybe that's it." I gazed dismally between my knees at the dirty floor. "I suppose I ought to get out of town," I said.

"Don't do it, kid. They know that kind of dodge, they expect it. Once you're out on the run it's all over. They've got you in their kind of situation."

I could see what he meant, and he was right. I said, "What

can I do, then? I need time to think, time to decide. Where can I go?"

"You been staying around your home, haven't you? That's where you got my note."

"I've been staying there mostly, yes."

"That's why you lasted so long," he said. "That's so dumb they can't believe it. You're on the run, and you know you're on the run, and they know you're on the run, and you stay home. They'll never think of it in a million years. You just stay to home, like you been doing. Don't go out on the street very much, if you can help it. And my advice is, unload that dough. It'll never bring you nothing but a bullet in the back."

"I don't know," I said. "I just don't know."

"You work it out for yourself," he said. "All I know is what I'd do. Just don't give the dough to the Coppos, that's all I ask. I hate the thought of them getting all that cash."

"They won't get it," I promised.

"Good." He got to his feet. "I can't hang around any longer," he said, and wiped his mouth again. "Say, what I told you, that's worth something, ain't it?"

"It is," I admitted. I took out my wallet again, found a ten, hesitated, put another ten with it, and gave them to him.

He took the money with a sardonic grin. "Three years ago," he said, "I was buying cigarettes at the Playboy Club with these, and telling the Bunny keep the change. You never know, kid, you never know how things'll turn out."

"I guess not," I said.

He scampered away across the terminal. I watched him, and when he was a good distance away I got up and followed him. There was a lot he'd already told me, but I had the suspicion there was also a lot more Professor Kilroy *hadn't* told me. I wanted to know more about him.

At first I thought he suspected he was being followed, the

way he kept looking around, and the fact that he was wandering around inside the terminal, doubling back on himself and hurrying along in great circles, but I kept well back and I'm sure he never did see me.

After a lot of this aimless rushing back and forth, upstairs and down, he finally headed for a bank of lockers, pulled out a key, unlocked one of the doors, and took out a neat new black attaché case of the kind being carried by half the men in the terminal. On all the others it looked normal, but on Professor Kilroy it looked incongruous. Carrying this unexpected bit of luggage, he headed for the nearest men's room and went on inside.

I waited outside. I waited for twenty minutes. Men went in and men came out, but no Professor Kilroy. Was there another exit? Dare I go in and look for him?

At last I did. There was no other exit and there was no Professor Kilroy. I looked all over the place, even peeking over the tops of stall doors—which got me called a few names—and he just wasn't there.

He wasn't there.

TWENTY-SEVEN

I came out of the men's room feeling baffled and uneasy and irritable. How had he done it? Where was he now?

As I stood there, with no doubt an expression of absolute stupidity on my face, a hearty man of middle age, robust appearance, good suit, nice pencil mustache, came up to me and said, "Say there, my friend, would this happen to be your suitcase?"

Distracted, I looked at the expensive-seeming blue suitcase he was holding up for my inspection and said, "No, it isn't."

"I just found it here," he said.

"Is that right?" I continued to look around the terminal, hoping to see the scuttling form of Professor Kilroy somewhere out there on the great floor.

"Do you suppose there's anything valuable in it?"

I looked at him, finally hearing what he was saying. "What was that?"

"I said, I wonder if there's anything valuable in here."

A great rage was swelling within my breast. I said, "Are you actually trying to work the lost-bag swindle on me?"

He blinked, and looked very innocent and very confused. "Well, of course not," he said. "I just found this—"

"If that isn't the last straw," I said. Enraged, I kicked him soundly in the shin, and went away from there.

TWENTY-EIGHT

I was being followed.

I had chosen to walk home, for a number of reasons. There was my normal reason of pot belly, of course, but in addition I wanted a chance to think about what Professor Kilroy had told me—particularly his idea that I should give the money away to save my life—and sometimes I could think best if I went for a walk. And I must admit there was also a third reason; in how many movies on the Late Late Show had I seen it happen, where the hero gets into a taxi he thinks is being operated by an ordinary hack, only to discover that the man behind the wheel is in actuality a hireling of the mob? More than I could count, that's how many. I'm sure Professor Kilroy would have called it paranoiac, but every taxi I saw seemed to glitter with a yellow evil, to be pregnant with malevolent potential. And never had I seen so many thuggish-looking cab drivers.

Therefore I walked.

And therefore I was being followed.

I had chosen to take Fifth Avenue, that being a broad and

well-lighted thoroughfare as well as more scenic than some of
the avenues to the west, and I had gone two or three blocks
before I became aware of them. They were in a long black Cadillac, the same car that had been parked across the street from
my apartment the other day. It was traveling now with only
its amber parking lights on, and there were black side curtains
drawn over the windows, hiding the backseat. In the darkness
within the car I could make out little about the driver other
than that he wore a chauffeur's cap.

Their method of keeping track of me was an odd one. They
would drive slowly past me and stop at the curb just short of
the next intersection. Then they would wait as I walked by
and went about halfway down the next block before once again
they passed me and came to a stop near the intersection.

It was more frightening in its own way than an out-and-
out attack; that sleek and silent car rolling slowly by me, its
tires crunching on the blacktop, then coming to rest like a
great panther just a little way ahead. The driver always faced
forward. The side curtains never moved.

Every time I went by I expected roaring gunfire from that
curtained window, or a sudden leap of burly thugs out the
doors, grabbing me up, hustling me into the backseat, taking
me for the final ride. But nothing happened, and our slow silent
terrifying game of follow-the-leader continued for block after
block.

What could I do? Obviously they were hoping for a time
when the sidewalk in my general vicinity would be free of
other pedestrians, so they could at their leisure and without
witnesses shoot me down or kidnap me or whatever they had
in mind for me. Failing that, I suppose they hoped to follow
me to the place where I was hiding out.

Ah, but the crosstown streets were all one-way, and maybe
that was my salvation. Coming up was 36th Street, one-way

eastbound; if I were to turn right, to turn west on that street, how could the Cadillac follow me?

It couldn't.

Just this side of the intersection the Cadillac throbbed like a panther feigning languor. It had sidled past me again and slid to the curb and stopped. I walked on by it, feeling the old tightening of muscles in the middle of my back, and once again nothing happened. I came to the corner, made an abrupt right turn, and strode briskly away down 36th Street.

And behind me a car door slammed.

I looked back in time to see the Cadillac shoot across the intersection, headed south, no doubt meaning to cut across 35th Street and come around in front of me, cutting me off at the Sixth Avenue end of this block. Meantime, a bulky man in a cloth cap had come around the corner and was walking at a steady pace after me, his hands in the pockets of his leather jacket.

I walked faster, pulling ahead of the bulky man, but without hope of getting down to the other corner before the Cadillac could come around and seal it off.

Ahead of me, about the middle of the block, there was light spilling from a small luncheonette, the only store still open along this stretch. And except for the bulky man behind me, I was the only pedestrian in sight. My shoulder blades itched and itched, and I hurried toward the luncheonette. There I would find people, safety, an island of light. If worst came to worst, I could phone the police; there was at least a chance the call would be answered by someone not in the employ of the Coppo brothers.

At the far corner, the black Cadillac nosed around the corner, its amber parking lights like the eyes of a sea monster. It stopped down there, near the corner, waiting for me.

I was nearing the luncheonette, nearing it, nearing it.

I was half a dozen steps away when its lights went out.

I almost stopped in my tracks. I did falter a bit, but then I remembered the bulky man behind me and I hurried on again. Only the occasional streetlight now gave homage to the memory of Thomas Alva Edison, a great man who should have statues erected to him on every side street in town. Well-illuminated statues. Next door to all-night diners with large clientele.

As I came even with the luncheonette, out its door came a man wearing white pants and a black coat, a jangling set of keys in his hand. I promptly veered right, walked past him, and went on through the open door and inside. "Power failure?" I asked pleasantly, and strode on into the darkness.

"Hey!" said an outraged voice behind me. "Whatcha think you're doin?"

"Coffee and a cheese Danish," I said cheerily, and fell over a table.

"Come outa there!"

"Make it a prune Danish, then," I said, got to my feet, and fell over a chair.

"We're closed, ya numskull!"

"How about the flank steak, hash fried, and green peas?" I asked him. I was crawling around the floor trying to find some way to stand up without hitting my head on the underside of a table.

"What are ya doin? Ya wreckin the joint? Come *outa* there!"

"Oh, I get it," I said. "Everything I want's on the dinner."

"Out! Out! Out!"

"When's the Swede get here?"

He wasn't a literary type. He said, "Do you come outa there or do I call the cops?"

I was on my feet again, albeit shakily. "Nyaa nyaa," I said provocatively, "you can't catch me."

"Okay, buster," he said, came striding in after me, and fell over a chair.

In an attempt to circle around him, I walked into a wall, backed away from that into a booth, caromed off a hatrack, and wound up with my arms wrapped around a cash register. I felt like the ball in a pinball machine.

But at least I was up front again, with him no longer between me and the exit. I could hear him blundering around somewhere in the interior, falling over things and muttering, "Where are ya? Lemme get my hands on ya. Where are ya?" Apparently he was in too much of a rage to think about turning the lights on, which was fine by me.

I tippy-toed toward the door, fell over a planter—what was *that* doing here, full of artificial flowers with sharp points?— and went the rest of the way on hands and knees. Still on hands and knees, I peeked out around the corner of the door, and saw the bulky man leaning against a store-front window about twenty feet to my left. And the amber-eyed Cadillac parked down at the corner to my right.

But coming toward me from the direction of Sixth Avenue was a group of teen-agers, all talking at the same time, most waving their arms, moving in a compact mass as though enclosed in an invisible box. They may all have been boys and they may all have been girls and they may have been a mixture of the two, it was impossible to tell. They all wore slacks and jackets and were slender without any particular shape. Their hair was too long if they were boys and too short if they were girls. Their voices were changing if they were boys and showed they'd been smoking too much if they were girls. They all walked as though they'd just gotten off motorcycles.

I got to my feet, brushed myself off, and as the group drew

abreast of me I stepped quickly from the doorway, inserted myself in the middle of them, and said loudly, "Say there, gang, you hear the one about the centipede with athlete's foot?"

They paid absolutely no attention to me. They just kept walking along the same as ever, all talking at the same time, most waving their arms, the compact mass unaltered in the slightest by my presence in its middle. One of them on my left was relating the plot of a motion picture, another one a little farther forward was describing a coat he/she had seen at some airport, one to my right rear was discussing American foreign policy, one out front was talking about the advantages of the university at Mexico City, and one on the left fringe was giving an impassioned defense of the birth control pill.

The bulky man had retired into a dark doorway. All I could see of him as we trundled by was a pair of malevolently gleaming eyes.

The Cadillac slithered by and came to a stop down near the corner.

At Fifth Avenue my platoon turned right. I was still trying to confound the Cadillac with one-way streets, and Fifth Avenue was one-way southbound, so I parted from the group there, turning to go in the opposite direction, saying, "See you later, alligator," as a way of dating myself for them.

"See you, man," one of them called after me, which I thought was very nice.

The bulky man was after me again, but the Cadillac was hampered from circling the block once more by a red light facing it at Fifth Avenue. Still, no light stays red forever, unfortunately, and before I had reached 37th Street I heard the swoosh of it back there, setting off on my roundabout trail once again.

May I point out that throughout this entire time I was absolutely terrified? It was the spasm of panic that had kept me going so far, and I was now finding out about myself that panic had a tendency to make me manic. The shyness I had always assumed to be an integral part of my character appeared now to be excess baggage, to be hurled overboard when the going got rough.

But how much longer could I keep it up? They were chasing me both by car and afoot. As nine o'clock neared, the business and shopping district in which we were buffeting was busy closing down; soon the streets would be more or less empty, the last of the stores and luncheonettes would be closed, the traffic along Fifth Avenue would slow to a trickle. In all that darkness and silence and emptiness they could finish me off like a man slapping a mosquito between his palms.

I crossed 37th Street, looked down to my right, and didn't see the Cadillac yet in sight; more red lights, I assumed. I kept going north. Behind me, the bulky man had receded to almost a full block back.

As I crossed 38th Street, I glanced over my shoulder and saw the Cadillac streak across the intersection a block south, jouncing like an ocean liner in a rough sea.

Well, at least I was giving them trouble. As I strode briskly northward on Fifth, the Cadillac was forced to zigzag like a skier on a slalom; east to Madison, up a block, west to Sixth, up a block, east to Madison, up a block, and so on.

Fine. They might get me, but I'd take some of their gas with me.

But 37th Street was the last I saw of the yellow-eyed monster until I approached 40th Street, where I saw they'd decided not to play that game. The Cadillac was parked north of 40th Street, in front of the library, waiting for me to come to it.

Well, I wouldn't. I turned left on 40th Street, which was again the wrong way for the Cadillac, hurried along beside the library, and beyond it on my right there was the inviting darkness of Bryant Park. Too inviting; the bulky man and I might go in there, but only the bulky man would be coming out. In the morning I'd be found among the ivy, if someone didn't steal me before then.

I hurried past the park, turned right on Sixth Avenue, and made for the bright lights and movement of 42nd Street. Reaching that corner, I came across another group, and promptly joined in. This time I knew what sex they were but they didn't. They twittered at my arrival and made quite a fuss over me. "Well, look what we have here," one of them said, batting his store-bought eyelashes at me. "Rough trade."

All things considered, I suppose I'll have to accept that as having been a compliment.

"Where did you come from, honey?" another asked me. "You off a ship?"

It seemed all at once as though I were only a few seconds from a fate worse than death, so I took the other choice, extricated myself—with some difficulty—from the aviary, and entered a handy bookstore.

From one extreme to the other. This place reeked of heterosexuality; men with furrowed brows and furtive eyes flipped through the racks of girlie magazines and sexy paperbacks. There was a kind of shabbiness overlying everything here, as though no one connected with any part of this could quite afford even second best.

The store was narrow and shallow and full of silent browsing men who weren't meeting each other's eyes. I threaded my way through them, saw a smallish green door at the very rear of the store, made for it, opened it, and stepped on through as the man at the cash register up front shouted, "Hey! Where you—?"

I heard no more, because I'd shut the door again.

I was in a small bare empty room with a single fifteen-watt

bulb glowing sullenly in a ceiling fixture. Across the way was a curtained doorway. I went through there and into another small room, in which three men were standing around a table looking at a lot of pictures of naked women. They looked up, startled, saw me in the doorway, and dropped the pictures as though they'd suddenly caught fire. "A raid!" one of them shouted, and all three went tearing through a doorway on the opposite side of the room.

I paused to glance at some of the photos, saw that they were of men and women combined in activities which seemed anatomically improbable, and went on through the further doorway after the departed trio.

They were long gone; not even the sound of a footfall or a hoarse cry of despair sounded ahead of me. I was now in a long dim hallway with a door at the far end boasting a frosted-glass window. I made for it, found it locked, and turned uncertainly back just in time to see two men entering the hallway at the other end. One was the man who'd been sitting at the cash register in the bookstore, and the other was a tall and heavily built man in a maroon sweater. Both carried short lengths of pipe in their hands, and both seemed very stern.

Midway between us there was a closed door in the left-hand wall. Crossing my fingers, I dashed for this—apparently my two pursuers thought I was dashing for them, because they stood where they were and braced themselves—and wonder of wonders I found it unlocked. I ducked through, saw a flight of stairs leading up, and went up them three at a time.

Four flights later, I was winded and on the roof. This struck me as being poor planning; if any of the people now chasing me caught up with me, all they had to do was throw me over the side. I went near the edge, glanced over, and saw the street several miles below. Ooogg.

Yes, but. Over to my right, three or four buildings away,

was one of the 42nd Street movie houses. The building roof was the same height as this one, there seemed to be a fire escape or ladder of some kind leading down to the marquee, and alongside the marquee was a very tall ladder atop which a very thin young man was engaged in changing the lettering announcing the movies playing within.

While I considered the unlikelihood of what I was considering, I heard the roof door behind me grate open and I wasted no more time in idle consideration. Without looking back to see who had caught up with me, I took off across the roofs as far as the movie theater, and down the fire escape to the marquee.

I wouldn't say that I have an abnormal fear of heights, but that's probably because I don't consider a fear of heights abnormal. I mean, you can get killed if you're up high and all of a sudden you're down low. People who aren't afraid of heights are people who haven't stopped to think about what happens when you reach the sidewalk in too much of a hurry. I have stopped to think about it, and I therefore felt very small, weak, nervous, terrified and top-heavy as I went down those iron rungs on the front of the movie theater, expecting at any second to lose my grip, fall through the marquee like a dropped safe, and make an omelet of myself on the sidewalk.

Amazingly enough, I made it. The top of the marquee was some sort of thin sheet metal, painted black, which bucked and dipped and went *sprong* as I walked across it. Looking back and up, I saw the two men from the bookstore still up there on the roof, looking down; they made no move to follow me, but contented themselves with threateningly shaking their pipes.

The head of the young man atop the ladder was just short of the top of the marquee. When I leaned down and said, "Hello," he started with surprise and very nearly took himself and his ladder completely away from me for good and all. But he managed to grab hold of the marquee and steady himself, which was lucky for both of us.

"Excuse me," I said, swinging my legs over the side and cautiously lowering myself toward the ladder. "I just want to—"

He was holding on to the marquee with both hands and gaping at me open-mouthed, his eyes popping. Fortunately his feet were on the second rung down from the top, so it was possible for me to get a good footing on the very top of the ladder and then to shift my hold from the top of the marquee to the metal letter guides across its face.

"I'll just be a minute," I said, trying to reassure him, not wanting to get into any sort of argument or fight or anything up here on top of a ladder. "If I could just, uhh, just swing around—"

I went down a step, edged slowly around him, skipping the rung he was on and feeling with my right foot for the rung just below him. Our faces were inches apart, he still hadn't said a word, and he was staring at me as though his face had been frozen in that expression.

"Just two seconds more," I said. I was babbling and I knew it, and I knew he wasn't really listening, but I went on babbling anyway. Panic takes different people in different ways, that's all. Him it made freeze, me it made babble.

I was finally past him. "Thanks," I said. "I appreciate it, thank you very much, I'll go on now, you do what you were doing, I'll—" And thus, babbling away, I continued on down the ladder.

I was almost down to street-level when, above me, my in-advertent benefactor finally found his voice and shouted down at me, "Why don't you watch where you're going?"

TWENTY-NINE

For some reason I had a little trouble getting to sleep that night, and so didn't awaken Wednesday morning until nearly quarter of eleven. I dressed myself haphazardly, still somewhat under the influence of my dreams, which had consisted primarily of my falling from great heights into the open jaws of huge amber-eyed cats with faces like Cadillacs, and as a result had to try three times before I finally got on a pair of matching socks. But I felt a little better after washing my face and drinking a cup of coffee, and decided to begin my day by seeing what the mailman had to offer.

He had junk to offer, as usual. I carried it all upstairs, sat down in the chair near the fireplace, and started to read.

My Cousin Maybelle wanted to study at Actor's Studio. Citizens Against Crime (Senator Earl Dunbar, Honorary Chairman) was back with another request for me to help stamp out crime by giving them money. The *Saturday Evening Post* wanted me to put the Golden Disk in the YES pocket and get eighteen years of their magazine for twenty-seven cents. A self-sufficient blind person had knit my initials onto some cheap handkerchiefs, which were being sent along for my inspection. Some crazy company sent me a little square of clear plastic and the information that if I acted fast I could have my automobile seats completely encased in the awful stuff. The National Minuscule Mitosis Association needed my help to rid the world of this dread crippler.

I read each letter—and each initial—with a great deal of care, and then threw everything into the fireplace. Except the square of plastic, which I suspected might melt instead of burn, and in any case would surely smell bad.

The letter from Citizens Against Crime I almost kept, it seemed so specifically to be directed at me; in fact, I found myself wondering if Uncle Matt himself might have written it. "Dear Citizen," it began, "Have you ever been bilked by one of the estimated eighteen thousand confidence men currently plying their nefarious racket in these United States? Are you one of the more than three million annual burglary victims?" And so on. The rest was more general, but that opening sentence hit me where I lived. Have I been bilked by *one* of the eighteen thousand con men? Listen, Senator Earl Dunbar, Honorary Chairman and signer of this letter, I, Fred Fitch, Honorary Chump, have been bilked by *all* of them.

In went that letter, too.

A little later, as I was putting breakfast on, I found myself thinking about the money again, trying to decide what to do about it. Was Professor Kilroy right, did my only safety lie in getting rid of it, giving it all to some charity so the Coppo brothers would leave me alone? I had gnawed at that question during my sleepless hours last night without coming up with any useful answer, and now I was at it again.

The trouble was, the question had a thousand sides and each side had a thousand arguments for and against and maybe-maybe. I should give up the money because it was blood money, bought with murder and lies. But I shouldn't allow the Coppos to intimidate me. But they did intimidate me. But with all that money I should be able to buy some sort of protection for myself. But how could I trust anyone at all so long as I still had the money? But the money was mine, I should be allowed to do with it what I wanted to do with it. But I didn't really need the money, I already had whatever I wanted. And so on, and so on, and so on.

Well, there was one thing I could do with the money, if I decided to give it up. Donate some of it to every nut that sent me a letter. In no time at all it'd be gone.

But would the Coppos take my word for it?

More important, did I really want the Coppos to dictate my life for me?

Even more important than that, did I want the Coppos to *end* my life for me?

What did I want with all that money, when you came right down to it? I didn't want to live in Uncle Matt's apartment, or any other apartment like it. I had an occupation that suited me and that I would prefer to keep up with anyway; what would I do with myself all day if I didn't work? All the money could do was make me its nervous watchman, keep me permanently what Professor Kilroy had so accurately termed paranoid. With my record as a sucker, I could see a nervous breakdown within six months. So maybe, after all, I should simply find an appropriate charity, turn the whole wad over to them with a lot of public fanfare, and return quietly to the life I was used to and content with.

But doggone it, that would be admitting defeat! Pushed around by a bunch of thugs. Harassed, browbeaten and conquered.

And so on and so on, around and around and around.

So the heck with it. I would make no decision at all just

yet, I still had another string to my bow. It was my intention today to call upon Prescott Wilks, the attorney whose piqued and somewhat cryptic letter I'd found in Uncle Matt's apartment. I wanted to know what sort of legal services his firm had done for Uncle Matt, why Uncle Matt had terminated those services, and just what that veiled threat in his letter had been all about.

After breakfast I looked up Wilks' address in the phone book, and there he was: Latham, Courtney, Wilks & Wilks, 630 Fifth Avenue. That would be Rockefeller Center. Right.

I left the apartment just after noon, went outside, and ran directly into the arms of Reilly, who grabbed me tight, said, "*There* you are, you damn fool," and hustled me across the sidewalk to an unmarked car.

THIRTY

I wasn't taken for a one-way ride to the Jersey swamps after all. Reilly drove me to a police station and marched me inside.

"I get a phone call," I said.

"Later," he said.

He went with me to the cells at the back, and watched me locked away. "I'm doing this for your own good," he said.

"I want my phone call," I said.

He shook his head and went away.

I made a great deal of noise for a while, shouting, rattling the barred door of my cell and so on, but no one paid any attention to me at all, so after a while I subsided.

It's a good thing I'd eaten a large breakfast; the lunch they brought me didn't even *look* edible. A phlegmatic guard came a while later and took the tray away again, and when I told him I wanted to make a phone call he didn't appear to hear me. In any case, he just picked up the tray and shuffled off.

A little after two o'clock another guard came and unlocked my cell. I told him, "I want to make a phone call."

"You got a visitor," he said.

"A what?" I peeked mistrustfully out at the corridor. Who would be coming to see me here?

"A visitor," he repeated patiently. "A nice young lady. Don't keep her waiting."

"Gertie?" I hadn't meant to say the name aloud, but I did.

"She didn't tell me her name," he said. "Come along."

I went along. I was taken to a scruffy-looking room with a long table in it, the table surrounded by chairs, at one of which was sitting Karen Smith. I looked at her and said, "Oh."

"Jack told me you were here," she said. "He doesn't know I'm coming to see you."

"Is that right?" I looked at the guard, standing in the doorway, not seeming to be listening at all to the conversation. I looked again at Karen, who didn't seem particularly dangerous sitting there with her coat open showing pink sweater and white skirt, and I decided to see what everybody was up to now, so I went over and sat down across the table from her and said, "Now what?"

"You're mad at me," she said. "I know you are. Is it that receipt?"

"Receipt?"

"The one you left on the coffee table. Neighborhood Beautification or something."

"Oh!" I'd completely forgotten that damn thing in all that had happened since. Now, remembering it, I also remembered where I'd gotten the money to pay for it, and I felt my face getting red.

Meanwhile, Karen was saying, "I feel as though I'm responsible for that. You didn't have any way to know it wasn't something I'd agreed to give money to, and it just as well might have been. So I feel as though I ought to give you your money back, and when Jack catches the man he—"

She was opening her purse. I began to wave my hands in

front of myself, saying, "No, no, please. No, that's all right. Really."

"No, I *want* to," she said. "After all, you were my guest."

"No," I said. "Please. Listen, you don't owe me anything at all."

"But I feel I do."

"Uh. Well, you don't. As a matter of fact—" I cleared my throat, and looked around at the guard—he seemed to be asleep on his feet—and finally I said, "As a matter of fact, I'm the one that owes you money. You see, I didn't have enough myself to pay him, so—uhhh . . ."

"But I didn't have any money there," she said.

"Well, yes, you did. Uhh . . ."

"Oh! The money in the dresser!"

I didn't meet her eye.

She said, "But how did you know about that?"

I studied my fingernails. They were clean, but I went on studying them. "I'm not normally like that," I mumbled, "I want you to know that. But there just wasn't anything to do there, I didn't know what to do with myself . . ."

"So you went through all my things."

I nodded miserably.

"Well, you poor man! I didn't even think! There we left you all alone all that time, it's a wonder you didn't have a fit or something."

"Well, it wasn't *that* bad."

"No, that was *terrible* of us. Is that why you left?"

I finally chanced a look at her, and her expression was serious but sympathetic. Apparently she hadn't chosen after all to look on me as a sex maniac who'd gone slobbering through her bedroom, for which I was grateful. I said, "No, that wasn't it. What happened, I got a phone call Monday afternoon."

"A phone call?"

"A man's voice. He said my name, and when I said yes he sort of chuckled and said, 'So there you are,' and hung up."

Her eyes widened. "The killer?"

"Who else?"

"Oh, Fred, no wonder you ran away!"

"They could have been calling from right down at the corner."

"Of course! But why didn't you let us know? Why didn't you call me in the evening, when I was home from work? Or why not call Jack?"

"The question I couldn't answer," I said, "is how they found out where I was. I still can't answer it."

With her eyes even wider than before, she said, "You mean us? Jack and me? Why would we—how could we—how could you!"

"How did they find out, Karen?"

"Well, I didn't tell them! I didn't tell anybody!"

Looking at her now, torn between outraged shock and sympathetic understanding, I was prepared to believe her. Karen Smith, I was now convinced, was no more than an innocent pawn in all this, as I was. I said so: "I believe you, Karen. But when I left there, how could I be sure? And how can I be sure now of Reilly?"

"Jack? But he's your friend!"

"I'm told a favorite line of my uncle's was, 'A man with half a million dollars can't afford friends.' "

"Oh, Fred, that's so cynical. Don't get cynical, please, don't let money change you."

"I'm changed already," I said.

"Jack is your friend," she insisted. "You know that as well as I do."

"Jack Reilly," I said, "is half con man himself, I've known that about him for years. That's how he knows so much how to handle other con men. Look how he's conned you."

Her face paled and she said, "What do you mean? What has he done to me?"

"All that jazz about the religious reasons," I said. "Reilly's got himself set up with—"

"I don't want to hear anything like that!" She stood up so quickly she almost knocked the chair over. "If you were a true friend of Jack's, you wouldn't say such despicable things! If you were a friend of *mine*—" She stopped, and bit her trembling lower lip. Clasping her purse in both hands, she fled from the room.

Now what had I done? What kind of idiotic wrong thing had I said this time?

Knowing exactly what I'd done, and wanting only to turn the world backward and erase the last three minutes and run through it all again without that stupid business about Reilly, I headed around the table after Karen, calling her name, going out the door after her and down the corridor.

The guard caught me halfway to the front door, and grabbed me in a very painful hammerlock. "Not so fast, my bucko," he panted. "You're a guest here, you remember?"

He trotted me back to my suite.

THIRTY-ONE

About three-thirty the corridor in front of my cell suddenly grew dark with cops. All of my favorites were there; Steve and Ralph and Reilly. Steve and Ralph had on their faces the slight smiles of an old vaudeville team waiting in the wings to go out and do their favorite number for the ten thousandth time, but Reilly looked sore.

When the guard opened the door and let them in, Reilly was the first one to speak, saying, "All right, Fred, you've done it this time. I don't know what smart ideas you've got about Karen, but you can—"

"What do you mean, smart ideas?"

"Turning her against me," he said. "I just had a bad session with that girl, and you owe me for that."

"Oh, stop it," I said. "I'm not the one with smart ideas about Karen. You come around here waving your finger at me, why don't you marry the girl or give her up?"

"That's none of your business, Fred. You just keep your nose out of my personal affairs."

Ralph cleared his throat at this point, saying, "Gents, if we could get to the business at hand here—"

"Which is the phone call I'm supposed to get," I told him.

Steve said, "Well, no, not exactly. We wouldn't be the ones to see about that. Would we, Ralph?"

"No," agreed Ralph, "that wouldn't be our department."

"We're more interested in homicide," Steve explained.

"I'm not talking," I said.

Reilly said, "Fred, will you start cooperating, for God's sake? What's the matter with you?"

"What's the matter with me? I'll tell you what's the matter with me. Somebody sold me out to the Coppo brothers, that's what's the matter with me. Somebody told them I was at Karen's place, and only four people knew that besides me, and three of them are in this cell."

Steve said, "How's that again, my friend?"

"You people are too funny to talk to," I told him.

Reilly said, "And me, Fred? Am I too funny to talk to?"

"I don't know what you are, Reilly. Until I find out, I don't talk to you either."

"Say it in plain language, Fred."

I met his eye firmly. "I don't trust you, Reilly," I said.

Before he could say anything in reply, the cell door opened and an elderly guard stood there blinking at us. "Which one's the prisoner?" he asked.

I was tempted to point at Steve, but I said, "Me."

"Come on along," he said.

Reilly said, "Hold on, there."

Ralph said, "What's up, my friend?"

"Gotta let this bird go," said the old man. "They's a lawyer out here with all the paperwork."

The last I saw of Reilly, he was standing in the middle of the cell with his face purple.

THIRTY-TWO

It was Goodkind. As lupine as ever, he stood out by the front desk with a smile of self-satisfaction on his face, waiting for me.

"I only heard about this an hour ago," he greeted me. "I got right to work on it."

"Thank you."

"You should have called me, I'd have had you out before this."

"They wouldn't let me use a phone."

"Ho ho?" His nose twitched, smelling a suit. "In front of witnesses? Nonpolice witnesses."

"No. They kept it in the family."

"Well. We'll have to talk about that later." He took my elbow, led me toward the door. "We have other things to talk about first," he said. "Important things."

I said, "Like the Coppo brothers?"

"Who?" He looked at me with such an absurd attempt at an innocent expression that I almost laughed in his face.

Instead, I said, "Or maybe Walter Cosgrove."

That got a reaction. Clutching at my elbow he said, "Where did you hear that name? Who's been at you?"

We were just inside the station house main door, and several uniformed policemen now trooped in, separating us. I went on outside, and Goodkind caught up with me on the sidewalk, grasping my elbow again, saying hurriedly in my ear, "Don't let them get at you, Fred. Keep away from Cosgrove's people. Don't listen to them."

"Everybody calls me Fred," I said.

"For God's sake, it's your *name!* Will you stop that, we have *important* things to discuss."

"We have not," I said, and then I shouted, "Help! Police!"

Well, of course, there we were in front of a police station, so we were immediately surrounded by nobody. There's never a cop around when you want one, including in front of the precinct house.

"Help!" I demanded. "Police!" I insisted.

Goodkind had released my elbow as though he'd just got word about my leprosy, and was looking at me as though he'd just got word about my psychopathic personality. "What are you doing?" he asked me.

"Calling for help." I demonstrated again: "Help! For Pete's sake, police!"

Abruptly we were surrounded by a trio of uniformed patrolmen, all of whom wanted to know what was going on. I pointed at Goodkind and said, "This bird just tried to pick my pocket."

Goodkind gaped in astonishment. "Me? Fred, are you out of your mind?"

"Okay, buddy," said one of the cops, and grabbed Goodkind the way Goodkind had been grabbing me—by the elbow.

Another of the cops said to me, "You'll have to come in and sign a complaint, pal."

"I can't," I said. "I'm supposed to meet my wife, if I'm late again she'll kill me. Let me come back later."

"Listen, pal," cop number two said. "If you want this guy held, you got to sign a complaint against him."

"I'll come back," I promised. "My name's Minetta, Ff—Frank Minetta, 27 West 10th Street. I'll be back in an hour." I started backing out of our little group. "In an hour," I said.

"We won't hold him any more than that," one of the cops warned me.

"I'll be back," I lied, and turned around, and trotted away down the sidewalk.

I got half a block when I heard a bellow behind me: "Fred!" I looked back and there was Reilly on the station house steps, waving his arms at me. Goodkind was yakking at him, clutching at his lapels, and the three cops were trying to wrestle Goodkind around Reilly and into the building.

It wouldn't take them long to straighten things out back there, and then everybody would be after me.

I started to run.

THIRTY-THREE

When Karen opened the door I said, "First of all, I want to apologize again."

"Don't be silly," she said. "We took care of all that on the phone. Come on in."

I went on in.

When I'd run away from Goodkind and Reilly and the police force, at first I hadn't been able to think of a place to go. The Coppo brothers and their mob might not believe a man would be dumb enough to hide out in his own apartment, but Reilly knew me and he could believe it with no trouble at all. That's how he'd gotten me the last time.

So where else was there? I wasn't sure I could get back into Gertie's apartment, nor was I sure it would be a good idea for me to be there; the mob knew about that place and might have it staked out just to be on the safe side. Since Gus Ricovic's occupancy, Uncle Matt's apartment was also too dangerous now.

Then I thought of Karen. She'd been angry at me when last we'd parted company, and I did want to get that straightened out, make my apologies, and whatnot. But besides that, she was apparently mad at Reilly now, at least according to what he'd said in that cell, and she just might be inclined to help me against him.

At any rate, I thought it worth a phone call, which I made from a stuffy phone booth in a dark and crowded drug store on Eighth Avenue. When Karen answered, I identified myself and launched at once into my apology, but she cut me off midway through the first sentence, saying, "No, Fred, you were right. I'm *glad* you opened my eyes, *glad.*"

I kept on trying to apologize anyway, but she would have none of it, so I switched to the other reason for my call, and she said she'd be glad to hide me out again, and now here I was.

"I'm pretty sure I wasn't followed," I said, as I walked down the hall into the living room. "That's what took me so long getting here. Back-tracking and whatnot."

"You're getting skillful at all this," she said, smiling at me. "Tell me what you've been doing since you went away from here."

"Oh, wow. You wouldn't believe half of it."

But she did believe it, all of it. She laughed at the idea of Dr. Osbertson knocking himself out rather than answer questions, she was wide-eyed at all I'd been told by Professor Kilroy, she shivered delicately at the discovery of Gus Ricovic, and she grew as incensed as I was at the treatment I'd been given in jail.

As I was finishing, the street bell rang, and when Karen went to the callbox to ask who was there we both heard the gruff angry voice say, "It's Jack. Let me in."

"No," she said, and walked away from the callbox.

The bell rang again.

I said, "Karen, listen, I really don't want to come be-tween—"

"Don't worry about it, John Alden," she said. She came over and sat down beside me on the sofa. As the bell sounded yet again she said, "Well, now. What shall we do this evening?"

THIRTY-FOUR

What we did mostly was talk. Or, that is, I talked, Karen being one of those rarities, a good listener. I think I talked so much primarily because I was terrified that if I ever did stop talking about my troubles she'd start talking about hers, and I really didn't want to hear the sad saga of Karen and Reilly and the hypotenuse.

What I talked about mostly was the money. "It's brought me nothing but grief," I said several times. "Nothing but trouble and worry. I don't see that it ever will bring me anything but trouble and worry."

"It just doesn't seem right to give it up," she said. "Not that you need it or anything, you're right about that. It's just—I don't know, it's as though if you give it up you've let the world beat you somehow."

"That's all right," I said. "I'm no fanatic, if I'm beaten I'll cry uncle."

"Well, what would you do with the money?" she asked me. "If you didn't keep it, I mean."

"I don't know. Give it to some charity. CARE, maybe, if

they promise to send packages around to all the city jails. Or the Red Cross. I wish that's what Uncle Matt had done. Let the Coppos take out their mad on the Salvation Army."

"It just doesn't seem right," she said.

That was the conversation, with variations, that we kept having all evening. In a way I agreed with her, it would be admitting defeat to give the money up. But that was pride, nothing but pride. I didn't need the money, I didn't really even want the money. To keep it simply out of pride, when to have it in my possession meant I was marked for death, was only foolish.

Oh, well. Another thing we did during the evening was not answer the phone. Karen did once, and it was Reilly, and she hung up on him. "My eyes have been opened about that man," she said to me.

Quickly I said, "I wonder if maybe the USO would be a good place to give the money?"

Then also I spent a part of the evening planning what I would do tomorrow. I would go see Wilks—it had been too late this afternoon by the time I finally got away from the jail—and I would also go to the newspaper library and see what I could learn about the Coppo brothers.

Would it be smart to get in touch with them direct? The Coppos, I mean. Maybe if I was to call them, explain to them I'd never even met my Uncle Matt, I hadn't asked for this money, I was intending at once to turn it over to my favorite charity, maybe they'd leave me alone.

And maybe they'd come wiggling through the telephone line and bite me on the throat.

Ugh. I gave up that line of thought at once.

I also spent a lot of time not saying anything in response to Karen's line about John Alden. I knew this girl only slightly, she was having an affair with a friend of mine—or at least a former friend of mine, time would tell—we'd never dated, and yet that comment about John Alden had certainly seemed like a suggestion that I make some sort of move in her direction. It was true I'd kissed her once, but the circumstances had been a little unusual and I didn't think the kiss should count as having been a step in any sort of courtship.

Besides, my attitude toward Karen was as confused and ambivalent as my attitude toward the money. In a way I wanted very much to follow up the John Alden line, but at the same time I was very much intimidated by her beauty and her—what shall I call it?—her sexual emancipation, if you'll excuse the expression. In any case, I did nothing, and Karen dropped no more hints on the subject, and our conversation seemed to travel along well enough without it.

A little before midnight it occurred to me to try phoning Gertie again. I explained to Karen, "I don't have much hope, but I try once or twice a day anyway."

"I'll make us fresh drinks," Karen said, and took our glasses out to the kitchen.

I dialed the number, it rang twice, there was a click, and a voice that was surely Gertie's very own said, "Hello?"

THIRTY-FIVE

"Gertie?"

"Fred?"

"Gertie, is that you?"

"Is that *you*, Fred?"

"You got away!" I shouted, and Karen came in from the kitchen to see what was going on.

"I been calling your place, Fred," Gertie was saying. "You at home, or where are you?"

"When did you get away? How did you do it?"

"I climbed out a window. You should of seen me: Daredevil Gertie, the Human Fly. I only got in here a little while ago."

"Gertie, you better get out of there. They're liable to come looking for you again."

"I figured to go to kak in the morning," she said.

Karen was waving frantically at me, and pointing at the floor with her other hand. I nodded at her, and said into the phone, "Gertie, come on over here. You'll be safe here, and we can talk."

"Here? Where's here?"

"I'm at Karen Smith's place."

"Oh, yeah? You and her are a thing, huh?"

"I'll give you the address," I said. "You got pencil and paper?"

"Hold on."

She was gone so long I was beginning to think she'd been kidnapped again, but at last she did come back and I gave her the address and she promised to be right over.

"Be circuitous," I said.

"What's that?"

"Make sure you're not followed."

"Oh. You betcha."

We hung up and I said to Karen, "She'll be here in a little while."

Karen said, "Well?" She had a very odd expression on her face, sort of waiting and humorous and fatalistic.

I had no idea what she meant, and therefore said, "Well what?"

"Fred," she said, and shook her head, and gave a long-suffering sigh. "I can see you're going to be a lot of trouble," she said. "I only hope you're worth it."

"Karen, I don't—"

"Don't you realize," she said, "that if you're going to kiss me before Gertie gets here you should start now?"

THIRTY-SIX

Time passed which is no one's business but my own.

Gertie arrived about forty-five minutes later, looking none the worse for her experience. She marched in, grinned at Karen, and said, "So this is the competition. I better lose a few pounds."

"I was just thinking I should fill in a little," Karen told her. "Come in, sit down."

"Tell me what happened," I said. "I thought they'd killed you."

Gertie dropped into an armchair, adjusted her skirt, plunked her patent-leather purse down on the floor beside the chair, and said, "If you ask me, they didn't know what they were up to. First off I figured like you, I figured it was all over for little Gertie. But no, they took me out to Queens some place, some cruddy section, little houses, all grimy, locked me away in a room upstairs. Then I figured, oh ho, it's the fate worse than death. Well, I've had worse than that. But no, it wasn't that either. All they did was keep me there, and talk a lot on the phone. They didn't know *what* they were doing,

224 ◇ DONALD E. WESTLAKE

those boys, they were a couple of lunkheads. I told them so myself."

"Two of them?"

"Yeah. The same two that grabbed me. They used chloroform on me in the hallway, or it would have taken more than two."

"Then that's why I didn't hear you scream or anything."

"You kidding? I didn't get a *chance* to scream. Listen, Fred, you ever hear of anybody named Coppo? Some name like that."

"You're darn right I did," I said. "Where'd you hear it?"

"That's who they were calling all the time," she said. "With my ear down by the keyhole I could hear part of what they said. Mostly bitching about having to keep guard on me, wanting to know what was up, what should they do with me, stuff like that. And the guy they talked to mostly was this Coppo. 'Lemme talk to Coppo,' I heard them say that a dozen times."

"There's two of them," I told her. "Two Coppos. They're brothers. I heard about them from Professor Kilroy."

That startled her. "Kilroy? That old buzzard's in town? I figured he was still down in South America some place."

"No," I said. "He's in town, and he got in touch with me." Then I told her about meeting Professor Kilroy, and what he'd told me about Pedro Coppo and the Coppo brothers.

When I was done, she said, "So it's the dough they're after, huh?"

"Professor Kilroy thought I should give it all to some charity."

"Give it all to putting those bums in the chair, you mean," she said.

"What about the police? Did you go to them yet?"

"Are you kidding? There's cops in on this somewhere, I heard that part, too. Those two lunkheads telling each other the only good thing about the whole caper was the cops were cooled off."

"I thought so!" I jumped to my feet, excited and angry at having my suspicious verified. "They're all around us," I said. "You don't know who to trust, you just don't know who."

"I know where *I'm* going," said Gertie. "First thing in the morning I'm headed for kak."

"That's what you said on the phone," I said. "But why go to them? What can they do?"

"They can maybe give me some protection," she said. "Besides, they're one outfit you *can* trust."

"How can you be sure?"

"From what Matt told me," she said. "Matt was no sucker, he knew when an outfit was legit or not."

Karen said, "What are you two talking about?"

"Kak," I explained.

When Karen continued to look confused, Gertie took over the explanation, telling her what CAC was and about Uncle Matt having been a consultant to them. Karen listened, and then said, "But can they really do anything? What kind of power do they have?"

"Some senator runs it," Gertie said.

"Senator Earl Dunbar," I said, remembering the letters I'd gotten from them.

"Right," said Gertie, "that's the guy. Senator Dunbar. The way I figure, with a senator running things they got to have something going. Besides, where else do we turn? We go to the cops, we're right back in the laps of the Coppo boys again."

Karen said, "But what can they do if the police are corrupt? There must be some honest policemen, why not go to them?"

"Honey," said Gertie, "the tricky part is separate the sheep from the wolves, you know what I mean? The cop on the take don't have a sign on his back."

Karen turned to me, saying, "Fred, do you really think Jack could be involved in something like that?"

"I don't know anymore," I told her. "I don't like to think of him that way, but I just can't be sure of him anymore."

"Kak's our best bet," said Gertie. "Fred, how come you didn't go there yourself?"

"It never occurred to me," I admitted. "They sent me a couple of fund-raising letters, so I guess I just naturally lumped them in with everybody else, out to take me for a dollar."

She shook her head. "You're a nutty guy, Fred," she said.

"Maybe so."

"Come to kak with me in the morning," she said. "You tell them the part you know, I'll tell them the part I know."

I hesitated, saying, "I just don't know . . ."

"What else are you going to do, Fred?"

"You're right," I said. I turned to Karen, saying, "What do you think?"

"I suppose it's best," she said doubtfully.

"Good," said Gertie decisively. "Then that's settled. Now the only question is, how slow a worker are you, Fred?"

"What say?"

"I want to know who sleeps where," she explained.

It took me a few seconds for the question to sink in, during which Gertie kept watching my face. Then I got it.

She nodded. "That's what I figured," she said, and got to her feet. "Come on, Karen," she said. "Let's leave Don Juan to his beauty sleep."

I think Karen could at least have had the charity not to laugh.

THIRTY-SEVEN

After breakfast, Karen announced that she was coming with us.

"No," I said firmly.

"I'll just call the office and say I'm sick today," she said.

Gertie said, "Fred's right, honey. Neither of us is liable to be very healthy to be near right now."

"That's all right," said Karen. "I'll help watch for them."

I said, "If this outfit's as good as Gertie thinks it is, maybe the mob has their headquarters watched or something. Anything could happen, and I don't want you mixed up in it."

"Fred," Karen said, "I think you're dramatizing this a little bit."

"Dramatizing? I've been shot at and followed and hounded, Gertie was kidnapped, for Pete's sake, my uncle was murdered, Gus Ricovic was murdered! If I'm dramatizing, what the heck are the Coppos doing?"

Gertie said, "Gus? What happened to Gus?"

"I'll just phone the office," Karen said, and went into the living room.

Gertie said, "What's this about Gus?"

So I told her about Gus, which seemed to shake her up quite a bit. "I can't understand it," she said. "What would Gus know? Why bump off Gus?"

"Somebody found a reason," I said.

Karen came back, saying, "Ready to go."

Gertie frowned at her and said to me, "Can't you talk her out of it, Fred?"

I just looked at her.

"Oh, yeah," she said fatalistically. "I forgot."

So we were an army of three as we marched out to the sunlight to strike our blow for decent society.

THIRTY-EIGHT

We'd walked less than a block when Gertie said, "I guess I must of been followed last night."

I stopped where I was, and without turning my head to left or right, said, "Why do you say a thing like that, Gertie?" The sun was shining, the morning air was crisp and clear and clean, and I couldn't have felt more like an exposed target if I'd stood on a sand dune in the Sahara.

"Because of the car half a block behind us," she said. "It looks like the same one they took me away in. Don't look around at it."

"I wasn't going to," I assured her.

Karen was standing on my other side, and now she leaned in front of me to say under her breath to Gertie, "Are you sure it's the same car?"

"Looks like it."

I said, faintly, "What sort of car is it?"

"Black Caddy."

"Uh huh," I said. "We're doomed."

"They won't do nothing out in the open like this," Gertie said.

Karen said, "We can get a cab down at the corner."

"No!" I said. "That's what they want. We get into a cab, and the driver's one of them."

Karen looked at me as though she might make a comment about dramatization again, but then she changed her mind and said, "Then what can we do?"

"Split up," Gertie suggested.

Karen said, "But wouldn't we be better off sticking together?"

"We're just a bigger target this way," Gertie told her. "If we split up, at least one of us'll get through to kak."

"Maybe," said Karen doubtfully.

"Gertie's right," I said, as though I knew what I was talking about. But at least if we split up there was less likelihood of anything happening to Karen. I had no illusions about which of the three of us the black Cadillac would follow.

Gertie said, "Start walking again. Casual, like we don't know nothing's going on."

We started walking again, stiffly, as though we knew exactly what was going on.

Out of the corner of her mouth, Gertie said, "When we get to the corner, we go three different ways. Remember, kak's office is at Rockefeller Center."

"I remember," I said.

As we approached the corner, I said, "Should we synchronize watches?"

I felt Karen give me a long and very slow look. "Guess not," I said.

THIRTY-NINE

The Cadillac was following me.

We had split up at the corner of 78th Street and Broadway, executing a maneuver like toy soldiers on parade, Karen turning left, Gertie going straight ahead, and me turning right.

The Cadillac also turned right.

At 79th Street I turned right again, and so did the Cadillac. It was keeping well behind me, but it was the same car, no doubt of it. I was sure the side curtains were drawn, too, the same as always.

Never had the sun seemed so bright. Never had the storefronts along 79th Street seemed set back so far from the curb, leaving such a wide expanse of sidewalk. Never had any block in New York looked quite so deserted at ten o'clock on a May morning.

We crossed Amsterdam Avenue, like an unobservant matador being followed by the bull.

At Columbus Avenue, 79th Street is blocked by the planetarium and the Museum of Natural History. There were bicycles parked out in front of both buildings. Driven by a wild surmise, I hurried across the street, but all the bikes had locks on them. Naturally. Everything in New York has a lock on it, much good it does anybody.

Across the street, the Cadillac was stopped by a red light. If I only had a vehicle of some sort, now was the time to get clean away from them.

A flock of boys on bikes suddenly swarmed around me, dismounting with the bicycles still in motion, kicking down the kick-stands, reaching with practiced knowledge for their locks. I looked around me and knew my chance had come.

The boy nearest me was very short, and stout, and wore glasses. I said to him, "Excuse me," and took his bicycle.

He looked at me without comprehension.

I got on his bicycle and rode away.

Behind me, there was a sudden flurry of shouts. Looking back, I saw the rest of the boys leaping onto their own cycles and setting off after me. And the Cadillac, finally having a green light to deal with, was nosing around the corner.

I faced front, bent grimly over the handlebars, and pedaled furiously around the museum and down 78th Street.

It had been years since I'd ridden a bike. While it may be true that a skill once learned is never forgotten, it is also true that if you haven't ridden a bicycle for years you're going to be dreadful at it. Particularly when you're driving down a sidewalk alive with garbage cans, young trees, fire hydrants and old ladies walking Pekinese.

How I threaded through all that I'll never know, but one way and another I did survive it, with a pack of howling bike-riding children in my wake, and with the black Cadillac snorting in muffled impatience at a red light back on Columbus Avenue.

At the far end of the block was Central Park, and I made for it like a bicycling bear headed for his cave. Ahh, but between me and the potential sanctuary of the park lay Central Park West, a broad avenue blazing with traffic. Buses, cabs, MGs, Rolls Royces, doctors in Lincolns, college boys in Ferraris, kept women in Mustangs, tourists in Edsels, interior decorators in Dafs, all tearing back and forth, all knowing they have sixty seconds of green light before the red light will return, all knowing that the unofficial world record is seventeen blocks on one green light and all trying to beat that record, and absolutely none of them prepared to deal with a nut on a bicycle abruptly crossing their bows.

But what was I to do? I was going far too fast—and was far too shaky—to attempt a left or right turn. With all those screaming children behind me—not to mention the Cadillac, which must surely have a green light of its own again by now—I dared not stop. There was only one thing to do, and I did it.

I closed my eyes.

Oh, the shrieking of brakes. Oh, the tinkling of smashed headlights against smashed taillights. Oh, the screams of disbelief and rage. Oh, the panic.

I opened my eyes and saw curb dead ahead. Some reflex left over from childhood made me yank up on the handlebars, so that the bicycle climbed the curb rather than stopping abruptly at it and leaving me to go airborne over the low stone wall and into the park. A similar reflex enabled me to turn right without capsizing. Down the sidewalk I raced, amid the strollers in the sun, leaving chaos, outrage, and crushed straw hats in my wake. So many fists were raised and shaking back there it looked like a mob of Romans come to hear Mussolini.

There was a break in the stone wall, and a path, blacktop, going into the park and sloping away downhill to the right. I turned in there, gasping for breath, still pumping furiously, and let the incline take me.

Beautiful. I could sit at last, and stop pumping, and feel the wind rush past my sweating brow. Down the slope I sailed, and even the yelping of the children still dogging my trail sounded suddenly remote and unimportant. I almost smiled, and then looked down at the bottom of the slope and stopped almost smiling.

A pond lay dead ahead. Possibly the most polluted body of water in the United States, it sported a necklace of beer cans, milk cartons, bits of wax paper, latex products, abandoned toy dump trucks, dill pickles, broken switchblade knives, half-pint muscatel bottles, cardboard coffee containers, copies of *Playboy*, brown shoes, and crib springs.

No. Please no.

I applied the brakes. That is, I applied what were the brakes on a bike when I was a kid, which is to say that I began to pedal backward. When I was a kid, if you were on a bike and you wanted to slow down you pushed the pedals backward against pressure and the bike slowed down.

Plus ça change, plus c'est change. Bicycles aren't bicycles anymore. I began to pedal backward, encountered no pressure at all, and kept on trying. Meanwhile, the bike was picking up speed. I was pedaling backward, the bike was going faster and faster forward, and that murky pond lay sprawled down there in front of me like an extra circle of Hell.

I couldn't think what was wrong. Was the rotten cycle broken? Why on earth wasn't I stopping? Furiously I pedaled backward, and more furiously I streaked forward.

The pond was scant feet away when at last I saw the little levers attached to the handlebars quite near my knuckles. Slender cables of some sort meandered away from these levers and disappeared into the bike's plumbing.

Could these be the brakes? I had no time to think, to ponder, to do anything but close my fingers about both those levers at once and squeeze. Hard.

The bike stopped on a dime, and gave four cents' change.

It's too bad there weren't any levers on me. The bike stopped but I did not. I sailed through the air with the greatest of ease, out over the olive-drab water, and seemed to hang there in midair while a peculiar yellow stench lovingly embraced me. Then I shut my mouth and my eyes, folded my body up in the fetal position, plummeted downward, smashed into the water, and sank like a safe.

FORTY

When I emerged, soaking and sputtering and spitting out candy
bar wrappers, on the far side of the pond, I looked about me
and saw the pack of boys splitting into two groups and circling
the pond on both sides, still intent on my capture even though
I no longer had anybody's bicycle. Is it good for little children
to bear grudges like that?

At the top of the slope I'd lately left I saw a cop, just making up his mind to trot down and ask me one or two questions.
I didn't have time for all that now, nor to be set upon by a
thousand enraged children, so I faced the other way and saw
ahead of me a jagged escarpment of bare rock. Perfect. Up this
it was possible for me to scramble, but no one would be able
to pursue me on a bike.

I had never in my life before been quite this wet, nor had
I ever run across water quite this slippery and greasy. My hands
and shoes and elbows kept sliding on the rocks as I climbed,
leaving green smears behind. But I did at last attain the top,
looked to my left, and saw across a bit of greensward the southbound lanes of the road that makes a long oval inside the park.

A traffic light was there—red, because all traffic lights are red—and among the vehicles hunched at the white line there was a taxicab with its vacancy light aglow.

Saved! I squished in a sodden dogtrot across the greensward, pulled open the cab door, collapsed on the seat, and gasped, "Rockefeller Center."

The cabby turned around in some surprise, looked at me, and did a double-take. He then leaned way over to look out his right side window toward the direction from which I'd come, saying, "It's raining?"

"The light's green," I said.

He immediately straightened, tromped the accelerator, and we joined the race to the next red light. On the way, he said, in a reasonable tone, "It ain't raining here."

"This isn't rain," I said, very near the end of my rope. "I had some trouble."

"Oh," he said.

He was quiet for two more red lights, but while we were stopped at the third he turned around with a peculiar expression on his face and said, "I hope you don't mind me pointing this out, mister, but you smell something awful."

"I know," I said.

"I would go so far as to say you stink," he told me.

"The light's green," I said.

He faced front, gunned, and off we went again. I sat in the rear of the cab and spoiled.

"You get some nuts," the driver decided. Since he didn't appear to have been talking to me, I made no reply.

FORTY-ONE

The elevator operator at Rockefeller Center didn't like my aroma much either. The CAC headquarters were on a very high floor, so that we spent a lot of time together, comparatively speaking; when I left, he was looking around his elevator for a window to open.

The door I wanted had no name on it, only a number. I entered and found myself in a small and scruffy reception room, with a receptionist at a desk and with Gertie and Karen reading respectively *Holiday* and *Time* on a bench to my right.

They both leaped to their feet at my entrance. Karen came running toward me, arms outstretched, saying, "Darling! I was so—" And recoiled.

"I'm sorry," I said.

Gertie looked at me, wide-eyed. "Wha'd you do?" she asked me. "Hide out in the sewer?"

"I had a little trouble," I said.

The receptionist said, "Sir, is that—is that you? The smell. Is it you?"

"I couldn't go back to the apartment," I said. "I'd just managed to get away."

The receptionist went over and opened the window all the
way.

I said, "Excuse me." I walked over to the window—the
receptionist circled around me like a dog avoiding a horse—
took off my jacket and tie, and flung them out into the world.
Then, facing the room, I told the three women, "I'll stay here
by the window."

The receptionist said to Gertie, "Is this the man you were
waiting for?" She sounded as though she couldn't believe the
answer would be yes.

But it was. "That's him," Gertie admitted. "But he ain't
always quite that bad."

"Maybe I can get you something else to wear," the receptionist told me, and hurried from the room.

Karen, keeping her distance, said, "I was so worried about
you, Fred. You didn't get here, and you didn't get here."

"I had some trouble," I said, for the millionth time, thereby
managing the difficult feat of overstating an understatement.

"I wanted to phone the police," Karen told me. "But Gertie
was sure you'd make it."

"I'm not sure I was right," said Gertie.

The receptionist came back at that point, carrying a white
laboratory smock, saying, "This is all I could find, sir."

"Thank you," I said. "Anything." I headed toward her.

Quickly she put the smock down on a chair and retreated
to the other side of the room.

It's discouraging to be a pariah. Feeling very hangdog, I
went over and picked up the smock and asked the receptionist
to direct me to the men's room. She did, and I left them, taking
my green miasma with me.

In a stall in the men's room I stripped down to the skin and put on the smock, which was—happily—too large for me. My hands disappeared inside the sleeves, and the bottom of the smock reached to my shins. I rolled the sleeves up till I could see my hands, and then went over to a sink and washed as best I could, patting myself dry with paper towels. At one point a portly man smoking a cigar came in, looked at me, made a U-turn, and went out again.

My clothing was ruined, all of it, even my shoes. I threw everything into the trash can and then, wearing nothing but my smock, I padded barefoot back down the corridor to the offices of CAC.

The door was propped open, held by a Manhattan phone book. Both windows were open wide. A faint trace of my previous perfume still hung at nose-level in the air.

This time everybody was pleased to see me. Or maybe amused to see me. In any case, they all smiled broadly when I came into the room. Karen said, "Oh, that's much better, Fred. Come sit down beside me."

The receptionist spoke briefly into the phone and then told us, "Our Mr. Bray will see you in just a few minutes."

"Thank you," we said.

Karen said, "Tell me what happened to you, Fred."

Gertie said, "You looked like they tried to drown you in garbage. Nobody's *that* mean."

I told them about my getaway. Karen tried to keep a straight face and failed. Gertie didn't even try.

"I'll laugh tomorrow," I said shortly, picked up a *Kiplinger* magazine, and read about life among the rest of the paranoids.

A few minutes later a very distinguished-looking man came in—gray hair, fawn topcoat, well-fed look—and said to the receptionist, "Ah, there, Mary, is Callahan in?"

"Good morning, Senator," she said. "No, he had to see the

Commissioner this morning. Did he expect you?"

"No, I just thought I'd drop by, see how things are doing."
He looked at his watch. "When did he expect to be back, did
he say?"

"No later than eleven-thirty, he said. I think he meant it
this time."

The Senator laughed, saying, "We'll take him at his word,
I think. I'll wait." He turned toward the bench where we were
sitting, and apparently took a good look at us for the first time:
two comely women of wildly disparate types, and sitting between them like a hospital patient waiting for the operation
on his gall bladder a sort of sheepish madman in white coat
and bare feet.

Political training has probably never come in handier. The
Senator's smile turned glassy for barely a second, and other
than that he gave no visible reaction at all. Recovering, he gave
the three of us the sort of blank cheerful smile an outgoing
man always offers when taking a seat with others in a waiting
room. I gave him back a weak version of the same smile, while
Karen studied the floor and Gertie studied the ceiling. Then
for a while the four of us sat there with magazines open in
front of us, like a surrealist's painting.

Finally the door to our right opened and a harried-looking
young man in shirt sleeves came out. He had a pencil behind
one ear, his collar was open, and his tie was loose. He gave me
a brief odd look, and then said, "Hello, Senator! Nice to see
you again."

The Senator stood up, and they shook hands. The Senator
said, "Good to see you, Bob. I believe these people have been
waiting."

"Yes, of course." Bob now turned his full attention on us.
"I'm terribly sorry to keep you waiting, folks," he said. "We're

a little understaffed around here. You said something about reporting a crime?"

"A whole box full of crimes," Gertie told him. "Murder, kidnapping, attempted murder, bribing cops, you name it."

Bob seemed a little taken aback. Chuckling a bit, he said, "That's quite a list, madam. Have any idea who's been doing all this?"

"Two brothers named Coppo."

The Senator suddenly burst out, "The Coppos again! They're becoming a two-man crime wave, Bob."

"You can say that again," said Gertie.

The Senator said, "Bob, with your permission I'd like to sit in on this interview." He turned to me. "That is, if you wouldn't mind."

Gertie said, "You're Senator Dunbar, aren't you?"

He smiled acknowledgment. "Former Senator, I'm afraid. Otherwise, guilty as charged."

"You run this outfit."

"Honorary Chairman only," said the Senator, smiling graciously. "A mere figurehead."

"You can sit in as far as we're concerned," Gertie said, and turned to me. "Right, Fred?"

"Of course," I said. I was pleased to have him; if we could get somebody important interested right away, it couldn't hurt and it might even help.

"Then come along," said the Senator. "You lead the way, Bob."

We all trooped on into Bob's tiny office, settled ourselves in chairs, and for the next twenty minutes Gertie and Karen and I told our combined story.

FORTY-TWO

"That," said the Senator, "is one of the most incredible stories I've ever heard."

"Well, it's all true," said Gertie. "Every word of it."

"Oh, I believe you," the Senator assured her. "I merely mean that it is incredible to me that in this day and age this sort of thing can still be permitted to go on. Vendettas, mob killings, kidnappings of innocent individuals from their very doorsteps—no, it's unforgivable."

"The question is," I said, "is it stoppable."

The Senator turned to me. "I wish I could tell you, Mr. Fitch," he said, without my having to ask him not to call me Fred, "that it is stoppable, that an easy solution awaits you here in this office. But I'm afraid I can't. We already have an extensive file on the Coppo brothers, I believe they're in our top ten—Bob?"

"Numbers seven and eight, I believe," said Bob seriously.

"Not that it matters," the Senator said, "unless we can show results. But we want those two, we want to see them behind bars. We have our top ten here, the same as the FBI.

All it means is, those are the criminals we concentrate on. Buy information when we can, try to find witnesses who are willing to testify—"

"Well, we're willing to testify," Gertie said. "Aren't we, Fred?"

"Of course," I said.

"Ah, well," said the Senator, "but it isn't really that easy. The Coppo brothers can afford the best attorneys, you know. And what do you have, really, to bring into court against them? What proof?" He turned to me. "You have the word of a dubious character, someone calling himself Professor Kilroy, whom you can't even produce to verify what he told you. Hearsay, nothing more."

"But the shots at me," I said. "The car that followed me. The phone calls."

"Proof," the Senator said. "You have no proof, no witnesses, no corroboration." He smiled sadly, and leaned toward me, saying, "I'm sorry, Mr. Fitch, I truly am, but these are facts I'm telling you. Our legal system does seem to offer more protection to the criminal than to his victim, but a democracy could hardly operate otherwise."

"Why not?" Gertie demanded. "Why not just toss bums like those Coppos in jail and get 'em out of the way?"

"Would you really want to do that, Miss Divine? Let's change the words from criminal and victim to accused and accuser. A small exercise in semantics, but notice how everything changes. Our legal system offers more protection to the accused than to the accuser. Would you truly want it any other way?"

"I know what you mean, Senator," I said, "and I suppose you're right. But that's abstraction, and I'm here in the concrete." I laughed self-consciously and said, "Maybe with my feet in the concrete."

"I sympathize, Mr. Fitch," he said, "and I wish I could offer you a brighter prospect, but it would be unfair. You see how understaffed we are here, and even with a full staff, and adequate financing, we could hardly do more than scratch the surface. Oh, we might dispatch our top ten, but there's always ten more behind them, and ten more behind them. Believe me, Mr. Fitch, the criminal statistics are frightening."

"It isn't just the statistics," I said.

Gertie said, "What about *me* on the witness stand? I was kidnapped, that isn't any hearsay."

The Senator smiled sadly at her. "Again, have you any proof? Witnesses? Did the Coppo brothers themselves kidnap you, and could you identify them?"

"The guys that guarded me called the Coppos on the phone."

"Can you prove that? The use of a name doesn't prove a thing, Miss Divine." The Senator sat back and spread his hands. "Forgive my taking the role of the devil's advocate, but I do want you to see what we're up against. The enemy is an elusive one, and well represented by counsel."

"What does it take to win?" Karen asked.

"To be honest," he said, "it takes money. Most of our success has come as a result of information bought and paid for. For instance, if we could know for certain which police officers have been corrupted by the Coppo gang, we could bypass them, go to the honest officers, arrange traps to catch the bribe-taking police red-handed. If we could buy from informants, for instance, the names of the two men who kidnapped Miss Divine, if we could offer one of them an inducement to turn state's evidence—" He spread his hands. "We can do it," he said, "but only a little at a time. We chop off the tentacles, slowly, but the head seems always to remain."

"And meanwhile," Gertie said, "the Coppos are still after Fred and me."

"All I can suggest," the Senator said, "is that you leave the city, perhaps even leave the country, until such time as these criminals have been put safely behind bars."

Karen said, "But what if they never *get* behind bars?"

"I really don't know what to tell you," the Senator said.

I had been mulling things over the last couple of minutes, and now I said, "Senator, could you use a donation?"

He smiled wistfully. "We could always use donations," he said.

"I've got one for you," I said.

Both women were looking at me oddly. Karen said, "Fred, what are you going to do?"

"I'm giving it away," I told her. "Here's my good cause, putting people like the Coppo brothers behind bars."

The Senator said, "Mr. Fitch, what are you driving at?"

Karen said, "Fred, don't!"

But I was determined. "Your organization gets the whole thing," I told the Senator. "Three hundred thousand dollars. I don't want the damn stuff, and it can do you people a lot of good."

FORTY-THREE

Of course, they all tried to talk me out of it. Karen just kept doggedly telling me not to do it, while Gertie was vehement, telling me I was crazy, nobody in his right mind would give away three hundred grand, and so on. The young man, Bob, kept saying, "You don't want to do this on the spur of the moment, Mr. Fitch." And the Senator said such things as, "You really should think this over, you know," and, "Why don't you talk to your clergyman first, see what he has to say," and, "You don't want to do something today you'll regret tomorrow."

But I knew what it was I wanted. I'd suspected for a couple of days that I wasn't going to be keeping the money, that the only thing left was to decide where was the best place to donate it. And when we'd come in here, when I'd seen this place and heard the Senator talk, I'd known then where my money could do the most good.

My money. But it wasn't my money, not really. I'd inherited under false pretenses, surely; if Uncle Matt had known the kind of goofball and born mark I am he would hardly have left me in charge of his ill-gotten loot. And it wasn't Uncle Matt's money, any more than mine, because he too had gotten it under false pretenses, stolen it from a man who'd ended his life as a result. If it belonged to anybody, really, it was the heirs of Pedro Coppo, his two sons. But the idea of giving those crooks any of the money just stuck in my craw; they were worse than Uncle Matt, worse than any con man. A con man may pick you for a dollar or a hundred dollars, but when he goes away he's hurt nothing but your pocketbook. He doesn't beat people up, or kidnap them, or kill them.

No, here was the best place for blood money. Let it go to the Citizens Against Crime, let it do good for a change. Let it put the Coppo brothers in jail, let it keep them there the rest of their lives. The rest of my life, anyway, that was good enough for me.

When at last they saw I was adamant about giving the money to CAC, and about doing it right now, the Senator said, "Well, sir, I hardly know what to say. Your donation will do a great deal of good, I can tell you that much. And it's the sort of windfall we don't even dream about around here, do we, Bob?"

"Not hardly, sir," said Bob, smiling weakly. "Frankly, I'm stunned by all this."

"I suppose what you'll want now is a lawyer," said the Senator. "Would you like to phone your attorney from here?"

Goodkind? Oh, no. "Let's use your lawyer," I said. "He probably knows more about this sort of thing than mine does. All we have to do now is draw up some sort of paper for me to sign, guaranteeing delivery of the full inheritance. That way, if anything happens to me in the meantime, you can still collect."

"Oh, I'm sure nothing will happen to you," the Senator said. "In fact, I think what we'll do is send a team direct to the Coppo brothers to tell them about this. What say, Bob?"

"I'd like to do it myself, sir."

"Good boy. You and Callahan." The Senator turned back to me, saying. "All right, we'll get the organization's attorney right up here. Bob, would you see to it?"

"Certainly, sir." Bob got up from his desk, excused himself to the rest of us, and left.

Senator Dunbar turned to me and said, "I wonder if you'd be interested in a job with us here, Mr. Fitch?" He smiled and said, "We'll be able to add to our staff now, of course."

"I don't know anything about this kind of work," I said, but I was pleased and flustered at having been asked.

"What sort of work do you do?" he asked me, and for the next few minutes we discussed my profession as researcher and the possibilities of adapting that profession to something useful to CAC. I finally said I'd think it over, and then the Senator told us something about CAC's history and record, and some specific anecdotes about the activities of the organization. All in all, we chatted about ten minutes before Bob came back in and said, "All set, sir. I cleared the conference room for us, we'll have more space there."

"Very good, Bob," said the Senator, getting to his feet. He and I spent a few seconds bowing each other out the door, and then I gave in and went first. Karen and Gertie, both still disapproving, though silently now, trailed after us.

We crossed the reception room and went through a door on the other side, into a long and rather narrow room dominated by a gleaming conference table flanked by comfortable-looking chairs with wooden arms and red-leather upholstered seats. A man was standing at the far end of the table, with a black attaché case open on the table in front of him; he was taking papers and pens from it, and lining them up.

There was something immediately familiar about this man, but I couldn't think what. He was perhaps fifty, medium height, slightly stocky but not overweight in any real sense, well dressed; the sort of man you see at half the tables every lunch hour in midtown restaurants. Was that it, merely that he reminded me of a type? But why did I have this odd feeling that I had seen *him* somewhere before?

Senator Dunbar came around me, saying, "Ah, Prescott, good to see you again." He and the new man shook hands, and then the Senator turned to me, saying, "Mr. Fitch, may I introduce the man who has donated his legal services to our organization free of charge ever since its founding. Mr. Prescott Wilks, here's perhaps our greatest benefactor, Mr. Fredric Fitch."

Prescott Wilks. The lawyer who'd written the letter to Uncle Matt.

All at once I felt a chill in the back of my neck. Something was wrong somewhere. I was surrounded by smiling, amiable, *convincing* people; we were all sliding effortlessly down the chute together.

It was happening again!

Then Prescott Wilks came toward me, his hand outstretched, a pleasant smile on his face, and all at once I knew where I'd seen him before, and that meant I knew who he was, and that meant . . .

"Professor Kilroy!" I shouted. "You're Professor Kilroy!"

FORTY-FOUR

I was surrounded by blank stares of incomprehension, but I didn't care. I felt as though a great fog were suddenly lifting and all at once the landscape was clear all around me.

"He is!" I told everybody, told myself. "He put on a fake beard and a fright wig and those glasses, he dirtied his face, he put on old clothes that were too big for him to make him look smaller and scrawnier, he walked funny, he talked with that gravel voice—"

Senator Dunbar approached me with a concerned look, saying, "Mr. Fitch, do you feel unwell? Has the strain—?"

"No strain at all," I said. "You know how I know? That attaché case there. You had it in a locker, with your regular clothes in it. You went and got it and went into the men's room and changed your clothes in a stall, and that's why Professor Kilroy never came out again. Because *you* came out! The minute I walked in here I knew I'd seen you somewhere, but I couldn't remember where. It was at Grand Central. You were one of the men that came *out* of that men's room."

Prescott Wilks offered me a beautiful imitation of a baffled smile. "I confess I don't follow you, young man," he said. He turned the smile to Senator Dunbar, saying, "Should I, Earl?"

Karen, looking troubled, touched my arm and said, "Fred? Are you all right?"

"This young man's been under a severe strain," the Senator said. "You've heard of the Coppo brothers."

Wilks nodded. "Of course."

"It's all a con," I told Karen. "The whole thing was a huge con."

The Senator went blithely along, explaining things to Wilks. "They've been making life difficult for Mr. Fitch," he said. "I don't think we could really blame him if he starts imagining things."

Gertie came over on my other side and said, "Fred, what's happened to you? You snap a cable or something?"

"I trusted you, Gertie," I said. "And you're in it with them."

The Senator said, "Bob, perhaps it would be best if you called a doctor."

"Dr. Osbertson," I said. "Let's get the whole gang here."

Bob didn't go anywhere. The room got quieter and quieter. Everyone was looking at me, and behind their worried, amiable, puzzled countenances I could see the beginnings of wariness.

Karen sensed it, too. Her hand tightened on my arm as she faced them, and the lines had been drawn: we two against the rest of them.

I said, "Prescott Wilks wrote a letter to my uncle. I've got it. I suppose the word for that is coincidence."

Gertie said, "Fred, you flipped. All of a sudden you don't trust nobody."

"And you weren't kidnapped," I told her. "That was just part of the buildup."

"Fred, believe me, I know whether I was kidnapped or not."

"You do, do you?" I looked around at the concerned false faces. "I'm going to find out what's behind all this," I said. "Walter Cosgrove has something to do with it, and I'm going to find out what."

"Bob," said the Senator, somewhat grimly, "I believe that doctor should be called at once."

"Yes, sir," he said, and backed hurriedly out the door.

"He won't call any doctors," I said. "He knows when the boat's going down. You take a look out there, you'll see him running for the elevators."

The Senator's smile was a little crooked. "I think not," he said. "Bob is a trusted assistant."

"Trusted?" I backed away, holding Karen's arm. "We're leaving here," I said. "Don't try to stop us."

The Senator said, "Are you sure the Coppos aren't after you? Before you go out on that street, before you expose yourself to the world, you had better be sure. You *were* shot at, you know. You were harassed, hounded."

For just a second I felt my grip on reality weakening, but I steeled myself and said, "That was you people. You were the ones shot at me. Professional mobsters don't miss three times, I should have thought of that long ago. You weren't trying to hit me, you just wanted to scare me. And it took three shots to attract my attention."

"I have no idea what you're talking about," said the Senator. "As for me, I've been on the West Coast the last three weeks, and can produce any number of responsible citizens to bear me out."

"Then it was Wilks," I said. "He ran the whole thing. He

took the shots at me, played Professor Kilroy, followed me in the car, called me at Karen's place—"

"That's the most fantastic thing I ever heard of," said Wilks. "I'm an attorney, not an—an—acrobat."

"I'll bet you seventeen dollars," I told him, "you were in your senior class play in college. In the drama society. I'll bet you've always had a yen for the stage. I bet you invest in shows. I bet you've been in amateur theater."

I could see my bets hitting home. Wilks turned to the Senator for help, and the Senator said to me, "Fortunately, young man, we're all friends in here, or these incredible charges of yours might have some serious results."

"Serious results? How's this for a serious result—it was Wilks that killed Uncle Matt!"

"Now, that's too much!" cried Wilks. "I have never raised a hand against a human being in my life!"

The Senator turned to Gertie, saying, "Miss Divine, this young man is your friend, isn't there anything you can do with him?"

But Gertie laughed and shook her head and said, "Forget it, Senator, the kid tumbled. You're not gonna get him back on the track now."

I said to her, "You admit it?"

"Sure," she said. "Why not?"

"You'll go to jail," I said. "That's why not."

"Not on your life," she said. "You got to have a lot of proof first, and you don't have a thing."

"You weren't kidnapped," I said.

"No kidding," she said. "And it wasn't always Wilks in the Caddy, sometimes it was me. You like me in my driver's hat?"

The thought of that Cadillac, so menacing, being driven by Gertie in a chauffeur's cap, with the curtainedback seat as empty as the inside of my head, filled me with humiliation and rage. "What about murder?" I demanded. "You think there's no proof there? Wilks'll pay for that, and so will the rest of you. Accessories!"

"Come off it, Fred," Gertie said. "Wilks didn't kill anybody. Look at him, he ain't the type. If this crowd was gonna kill Matt, they'd of done it years ago. He held them up five years, you know."

The Senator suddenly burst out, "I've heard enough! You people come in here with a story of harassment, we offer you our assistance, and suddenly you start making these wild accusations— If you don't leave at once, I'll call the police!"

"I'll do it for you," I said. "Come on, Karen."

We backed cautiously out to the reception room. Beside me, Karen seemed as tense as an overwound watch. Her face was very white, except for two small circles of high color on her cheeks. She gazed at each speaker in turn, and when no one was speaking she looked at the Senator, much the way I suspect the bird looks at the snake.

The reception room was empty, the receptionist having abandoned her post. Bob didn't seem to be around anywhere, either. I moved toward the desk and the phone.

The Senator had followed me. "I would prefer it," he said coldly, "if you would not make your personal calls on my telephone."

"There's other phones," I said. "Gertie? Are you coming with us?"

She grinned at me and shook her head. "Naw, I better stick here with these birds and get our story straight. See you later, Fred."

When Karen and I backed out, Gertie was still grinning at me, standing there flanked by Wilks and the Senator, both of whom were looking very grim.

I had the funny feeling Gertie was proud of me.

FORTY-FIVE

"Gertie's note from Uncle Matt," I told Karen as we waited for the elevator, "was a fake. They had to get her close to me so she could set me up for the con. She's the one told me about Professor Kilroy and about kak."

"I'm lost, Fred," Karen said. She looked dazed. "All of a sudden, everything is something else."

"I've gone through my life that way," I said. I began counting, saying, "How many parts did Wilks play? He took the shots at me. Then he was the rabbi. Then he—"

"The rabbi? Fred, *do* you feel all right?"

I said, "The day I got the call at your place, a rabbi came around to the door. Old man with a heavy beard, mumbling. They knew I was in the building, but they didn't know which apartment. So Wilks got out the makeup kit and kept knocking on doors till he found me."

"How did they know you were in the building?"

"Followed me from my place."

She said, "And you thought it was Jack, you thought he betrayed you. You owe him an apology, Fred."

"I know it. Back to Wilks. After the rabbi, he was Professor Kilroy. They couldn't take a chance on Gertie giving me the whole con, it might not ring true, so they filled in with Professor Kilroy. Then Gertie drove the car and Wilks was the man in the cap. And this morning it was Wilks in the Cadillac again."

The elevator door slid open. The operator and a half-dozen passengers looked at me in absolute astonishment. For just a second I couldn't think why anybody would look at me like that, but when I glanced down to see if my fly was shut and saw that I was still barefoot and wearing the laboratory smock, I understood. I felt my face light up like an exit sign. Looking as dignified and unconcerned as I could manage, I took Karen's arm and we boarded the elevator.

On the way down Karen said, "What do we do now?"

"Call the police," I said. "First thing."

But I didn't have to call the police. The second my bare foot hit the sidewalk of Fifth Avenue, I was arrested.

FORTY-SIX

That evening Reilly brought me some clothing and the news I was no longer to be kept in jail. I'd had a long session already with Steve and Ralph, about which the less said is believe me the better, and now they were done with me.

The meeting with Reilly was very awkward at first, with me apologizing and being defensive all at once, and he simultaneously understanding and swallowing rage.

"Fred," he said, "all I ask is you find the happy medium. First, you trust everybody. Then, you trust nobody. Can't you get in the middle someplace?"

"I'll try," I said. "I really will."

"All right, enough of that," he said. "That's behind us, that isn't what I came here for. I thought you'd like to know what else I found out."

"I'd love to know it," I said.

"I got most of it from Goodkind," he said. "He swears he would've told you if you'd given him a chance, but I don't believe it. I think he had another song and dance for you, something to cover the facts without giving the facts."

"Like Senator Dunbar and company," I said.

"Same style. Anyway, what Goodkind says, that money never did belong to your uncle. He didn't steal it or make it or win it or anything. You were right about Walter Cosgrove being involved in this; it was his money."

"He had to be involved," I said. "Dr. Osbertson knew him. Wilks obviously knew him, from the way he acted when I said the name to him while he was being Professor Kilroy."

"The way Goodkind got the story," Reilly said, "Matt was down and out in Brazil when Cosgrove found him. Matt was dying of cancer and he knew it. Cosgrove had to get half a million dollars into the States and into the hands of Earl Dunbar. Dunbar has influence, he could wangle some sort of pardon or amnesty for Cosgrove, so Cosgrove could come back to this country. Half a million was Dunbar's price, in advance."

"This is too complicated," I said.

"Not really," he said. "Not when you get down to the core of it. Anyway, Dunbar had this Citizens Against Crime gimmick, he's had it for years, a safe front for any money he wanted to collect without soiling his hands. The sort of cash a lesser politician would call campaign contributions. But Dunbar was smarter than that; money never went directly to him. CAC got it, and then he siphoned it off, leaving just enough to maintain the organization. That office you saw is the extent of it."

"But what about Cosgrove and the money?"

"Cosgrove gave it to Matt," Reilly said, "because Matt was supposed to die in less than a year, and he was supposed to leave a will in which he repented his evil life and left all his money to CAC to continue its good work."

"He double-crossed them," I said.

"He double-crossed them six ways from Sunday. First, by

staying alive five years instead of six months. And second, by leaving his money to you."

"That's why Wilks killed him then," I said. "Because Matt fired him, and he suspected a double-cross."

Reilly shook his head. "No. In the first place, Wilks desperately didn't want Matt to die until he found out what the cross was. In the second place, Wilks has a rock-solid alibi for the time of the murder."

"It wasn't Wilks?"

"Definitely not."

"Well, it wasn't the Coppo brothers," I said. "If there are any Coppo brothers."

"Oh, there are," Reilly said. "But they don't come from Brazil, they come from Canarsie. And they never had anything to do with you or your uncle or anybody else in this mess."

"But they're real," I said. "Just in case I should happen to look them up in the newspaper files, I suppose."

"Something like that."

"But all that complicated machinery they had working around me," I said. "Why go through all that?"

"They couldn't just go to you and say your uncle made a mistake, the money's supposed to be theirs. Dunbar was putting pressure on Wilks from one side, and I suppose Cosgrove was putting pressure on him from the other side. You had a reputation for gullibility, so they started setting this thing up, making it up as they went along, hustling you around as best they could. Also, I think Wilks enjoyed it. You were right about him, he's a frustrated ham."

"If I hadn't seen that letter from him in Uncle Matt's desk," I said, "I might never have tipped. I'd have signed the papers, and it would have been all over."

"It was close," Reilly agreed. "You're a born sucker, Fred, and a born sucker's worst enemy is himself."

"I'm getting better," I said. "I think I've learned something these last few days."

"Maybe so," he said, but he didn't sound convinced.

I said, "The only question is, which one of them killed Uncle Matt? And Gus Ricovic? If Wilks didn't, which one did?"

"None of them," Reilly said. "They're all clean. Besides, it wouldn't make sense for them to wait five years and then kill Matt. And besides that, they suspected he was up to something, and they hoped he *wouldn't* die until they found out what it was."

"Then who killed Uncle Matt?"

"I have no idea," he said.

I said, "I've been figuring it was all tied together, the con and the murder. But that was what they wanted me to think, wasn't it? Tying everything together."

"As best as we can tell," said Reilly, "there's no tie-in at all. Wilks and Gertie Divine simply used the fact of the murder to hang their con on."

"Oh, for Pete's sake," I said, feeling sudden relief. "In that case, I know who did it."

Reilly looked at me dubiously. "You do?"

"The elevator operator."

"The what?"

"At his apartment house," I said. "The night elevator operator."

"Fred, do you feel all right?"

"I feel fine. Listen to me. Matt used to play cards with the elevator operator, and you know Matt had to be cheating him, just naturally, not even thinking about it. But he was getting sloppy. Gertie and Gus Ricovic both used to catch him all the time, but they let him get away with it."

"You're sure of this?" Reilly asked me. He was looking less dubious and more interested.

"Positive," I said. "And that elevator operator is nowhere near as sharp as Gertie, so he never knew Matt was cheating him until the last night they played. Then when he caught him Matt must have gotten sore, maybe threatened to tell the management, and the management would fire anybody who socialized with the tenants, the elevator man told me so himself. He got frantic when Matt headed for the phone, and killed him. Hit him with a bottle, maybe, and took the bottle away with him."

"You're sure he and Matt played cards?"

"Positive. Gertie told me, for one. And the elevator man himself told me so."

"I don't think our people knew about that," Reilly said thoughtfully.

"Everybody was covering for him, because they didn't want him to get in trouble for socializing."

"But what about Ricovic?" Reilly asked me.

"That's the clincher," I said. "The only reason Gus Ricovic would have been in that building at that time was to talk to the killer, tell him it would take a bid of over three thousand dollars to keep him from selling the truth to me. I think Gus had an odd attitude toward life, it would never occur to him anybody might try to kill him, no matter what."

"The MO was the same," Reilly said. "Both hit over the head with blunt instruments."

"Elevator operator," I said. "I'd have seen it long ago if I hadn't convinced myself all this other stuff was tied in with the killing."

"I'll be right back," said Reilly. "I've got to make a call."

I spent the time while he was gone getting dressed, setting aside the laboratory smock with something less than reluctance.

When Reilly returned he said, "The boys are checking it."

I said, "What about Wilks and Dunbar and the rest? What happens to them now?"

"Nothing, unfortunately," he said. "There's no real proof of anything they did, no way to successfully bring them into court. Earl Dunbar won't be doing much to help Walter Cosgrove get back into the country, but that's about the best you can say for the whole affair."

"And Gertie? What about her fake kidnapping?"

"You're the only one reported her kidnapped, Fred. She says no, she was out of town is all. She never claimed to be kidnapped."

"So everybody's scot-free," I said.

"Including you, Fred," Reilly pointed out. "Try looking at it that way, why don't you?"

I tried looking at it that way.

FORTY-SEVEN

Two days later, on Saturday, I was in Gertie's apartment. She was making us a quick lunch before we went for a ride in my new car—she would be driving until I got my license—and when the phone rang she said, "You get it, honey, will you?"

It was Reilly. When he heard my voice he said, "Karen said you'd be there, but I didn't believe it."

"Why not? I told Karen when I talked to her—"

"Yeah, yeah, I know." Grumpily he said, "I suppose I owe you thanks for that."

"For what?"

"For talking to Karen."

"Oh," I said. "Heck, I figured I owed you something, mistrusting you that way. And it was pretty much my fault that Karen broke up with you, so I thought I'd see if I could fix it up again."

"I had it all wrong about you," he said. "The way I saw it, you were out to get Karen for yourself."

"Not me," I said. "In the first place, she's your girl. And

in the second place, she really isn't my type, and I'm not really her type. You're her type."

He said, "What do you mean, she isn't your type?"

"She's too—uhh—normal for me, Reilly. I'm more of a—"

Gertie came in from the kitchen, brandishing a tableknife covered with mayonnaise, saying, "What was that?"

"Just a second." I turned to Gertie, saying, "I hate mayonnaise."

"Not *my* mayonnaise. I make it myself, in a blender."

I made a doubtful face, and turned back to the phone. "You and Karen were meant for each other, Reilly," I said. Gertie went back to the kitchen.

Reilly said, "Well, I don't know what you said to her, but it did the job, I've got to admit it. There's no more trouble around here."

"I just told her," I said, "that you and she made a perfect couple and that men are like loaves of bread. Half is better than none. And when she said women also didn't live on bread alone I told her about the phallic significance of the staff of life and suggested that we invent our lives for ourselves anyway, so why didn't she live the romantic fantasy you were offering her, and she—"

"You did *what?*"

"It worked, Reilly," I pointed out.

"I don't know," he said pensively, "it shouldn't work." He sighed and said, "All right, never mind that. The other thing I called about, your elevator operator confessed an hour ago. You were right on all counts. He caught Matt cheating, got mad, swore some, and Matt threatened to phone the doorman and have him thrown out. They'd been drinking, the two of them. The elevator man grabbed up an empty bottle, clubbed Matt with it, and left. He dropped the bottle down the elevator shaft.

The lab boys are over there now, putting the pieces together."

"What did he use on Gus Ricovic?"

"Eight ball from the pool table. Ricovic knew about the setup, and guessed it was the elevator man who'd killed Matt. He asked for an offer better than three thousand, but the elevator man didn't have any money, so he took Ricovic into the apartment to talk it over, hit him with the eight ball, hid the body, washed the eight ball in the bathroom sink, and went back to work."

"Where'd he get the apartment key?"

"From Matt. So he could come in any time, to play cards, or bring booze, or whatever."

"So it's all cleared up."

"Right."

"Good. I'm glad to hear it."

"But what about you? I heard you were going to give the money away after all."

"I was considering it," I said.

"Why?"

"Well, mostly because it was ill-gotten gains. Blood money. And I'd gotten along all right without it for thirty years."

"So who gets it all?"

"I do."

"You what?"

"Gertie explained it to me," I explained to him. "She pointed out that I could still live my old life as much as I wanted, but much more comfortably now. Instead of paying rent on my apartment I could buy the house. That way nobody'll ever buy it to build a parking lot there. And so on."

"So you're keeping it," he said faintly.

"Gertie won't let me do anything but."

(Actually, what Gertie had said, more frequently than anything else, was, "Are you crazy? That's *money!*")

He said, "You aren't buying any more gold bricks, are you?"

"Not too many," I said. "I'm being a little careful."

"But not paranoid anymore."

"No, I don't think so. I'm trying for a balance."

"Glad to hear it. Is Goodkind still your lawyer?"

"No, I let him go. Uncle Matt hired him because he was a crook and they could get along. I fired him for the same reason."

"Who's your new lawyer? Anybody I know?"

"Oh, sure. You know him pretty well. Prescott Wilks."

"*What?*"

"Dunbar fired him, in a fit of pique. So I figured, there's a man that really hustles for his clients. So I hired him. I think he's going to work out all right." I sniffed. There was a very odd and unpleasant odor coming from the kitchen. Gertie's mayonnaise?

Reilly was saying, "You with Gertie for the same reason?"

I got a little offended at that. "Gertie and I," I said stiffly, "are good friends. She's teaching me some things."

"I don't doubt it."

"Listen, Reilly, just because a girl dances at the Artillery Club in San Antonio doesn't mean she has loose morals. Gertie is—"

"Whatever you say, Fred."

"Well, she is." The smell was getting worse.

"I'm sure of it."

"I've got to hang up now, Reilly," I said. "There's something wrong here. I'll talk to you later."

I hung up, and started toward the kitchen, and met Gertie and a cloud of smoke coming out. I said, "What's going on?"

"You tell me, buster," she said, giving me the gimlet eye.

"Me? Why me?"

"Ten minutes ago I started to preheat the oven. I just looked in there now, and you know what's in there?"

"It smells like naugahyde," I said.

"I don't know about any of those places," she said. "All I know is, in my oven there's a burning Bible."

"A bur—" I said, and the last of the cons perpetrated on me suddenly opened like a flower before my eyes.

Of course, it was too late to stop payment on the check. But at least it gave us a neat ending, and that's one thing all good cons must have.

A neat ending.